Blinded
–by the–
Shining Path

This book is presented by
TAU UPSILON OMEGA

Ivy READING ACADEMY

Trailblazer Books

*Hero Tales: A Family Treasury of True Stories
From the Lives of Christian Heroes* (Volumes I, II, III, & IV)

*Curriculum guide available.
Written by Julia Pferdehirt with Dave & Neta Jackson.   02C

Blinded
–by the–
Shining Path

Dave & Neta Jackson

Illustrated by Anne Gavitt

BETHANY HOUSE PUBLISHERS
MINNEAPOLIS, MINNESOTA 55438

Published by Bethany House Publishers
A Ministry of Bethany Fellowship International
11400 Hampshire Avenue South
Bloomington, Minnesota 55438
www.bethanyhouse.com

Printed in the United States of America by
Bethany Press International, Bloomington, Minnesota 55438

Library of Congress Cataloging-in-Publication Data

Jackson, Dave.
 Blinded by the shining path : Rómulo Sauñe / by Dave & Neta Jackson ; illustrations by Anne Gavitt.
  p. cm. — (Trailblazer books)
 Summary: A young Quechua Indian learns firsthand the courage of committed Christians when Rómulo Sauñe, a missionary, turns the local people away from the hate and terror of the Shining Path, a guerrilla group.
 ISBN 0-7642-2233-3
 1. Sauñe, Rómulo, d. 1989—Juvenile fiction. [1. Sauñe, Rómulo, d. 1989—Fiction. 2. Missionaries—Fiction. 3. Terrorism—Fiction. 4. Quechua Indians—Fiction. 5. Indians of South America—Peru—Fiction. 6. Peru—Fiction. 7. Christian life—Fiction.] I. Jackson, Neta. II. Gavitt, Anne, ill. III. Title. IV. Series: Jackson, Dave. Trailblazer books.
PZ7.J132418 Bl 2002
[Fic]—dc21

                    2002009986

Details about Rómulo Sauñe (pronounced ROW-muh-low SOUW-nyay) and his ministry are true, including the young man who came to assassinate him late one night but came back the next day with a very different purpose. However, a man looking like Alfredo Garcia (not his real name) was arrested as a suspected member of the Shining Path two weeks later. Rómulo believed he died in a prison riot several months after that, but there was no proof. Alfredo's brother, mother, and his role in capturing Abimael Guzmán are all fictional.

Though there are many villages in Peru called Santa Rosa, the one in this story is fictional. The incident involving Pastor Jorge and the dynamited chair, however, is true.

Find us on the Web at . . .

TrailblazerBooks.com

Meet the authors.

Read the first chapter of each book—with the pictures.

Track the Trailblazers around the world on a map.

Use the historical timeline to find out what other important events were happening in the world at the time of each Trailblazer story.

Discover how the authors research their books, and link to some of the same sources they used, where you can learn more about these heroes.

Write to the authors.

Explore frequently asked questions about writing and Trailblazer books.

Just point your browser to *www.trailblazerbooks.com*

CONTENTS

DAVE AND NETA JACKSON are a full-time husband/wife writing team who have authored and coauthored many books on marriage and family, the church, relationships, and other subjects. Their books for children include the TRAILBLAZER series and *Hero Tales,* volumes I, II, III, and IV. The Jacksons make their home in Evanston, Illinois.

Chapter 1

The Hit That Missed

The music drifting from the small adobe church reminded fourteen-year-old Alfredo of happier days, days high in the Andes Mountains, where he sat alone and played his flute while the wind howled among the rocky peaks.

Absentmindedly he reached for the flute he had carried so long in his pocket, only to find the cold iron of a pistol. In the evening's dimming light, he glanced at his two companions, as though they might read his mind. He did not play his flute anymore. He was a soldier with the Shining Path guerrillas and could not afford the luxury of music.

While he sat leaning against a tree near the front door of the old church,

Alfredo's two companions, Juan and Rhony, dozed beside him, their heads pillowed on a blanket roll.

Rhony roused himself and muttered, "*Karun purina pisiqtaq k'oqao.*"

"Speak Spanish," snapped Juan. "I don't understand your Quechua language."

Rhony rolled his eyes. "I said, this is a lot of work without much to eat." Rhony and Alfredo were Peruvian Indians from mountain villages. Juan was from the city of Lima and spoke only Spanish.

Rhony raised up on an elbow and looked at Alfredo. "When will this preacher of yours be coming out?"

Alfredo shrugged and looked at the moon, which was just coming up over the snow-capped mountains to the east. "Sometimes they sing until midnight. Who knows?"

"Midnight?" Juan sat up and looked toward the church. "Then how come we came so early?"

"So nobody would notice us. We're just some poor Indians sitting under a tree."

"Yeah," said Rhony, "with our rifles rolled up in an old blanket."

"Right." Alfredo glanced at the dark roll his comrade had been resting on. "No one can tell what's in that."

"Maybe no one is suspicious now. But what about afterward? What about after we shoot that preacher? Then they will think back, and someone will say, 'Yeah, I remember *kimsa runas* under that tree.'"

Juan punched Rhony. "Speak Spanish!"

"Three guys," snapped Rhony. "Someone will remember three guys sitting under this tree with a long blanket roll that could have concealed guns."

"So what?" said Alfredo. "They won't remember who we are." He paused and studied Rhony. "You sound like you're scared. You want out?"

Rhony sighed—"No!"—and lay back down. Juan relaxed again, as well.

Alfredo leaned against the tree. It was strange, him asking Rhony if he wanted out. No one got out of the Shining Path alive. His brother had learned that the hard way. So why had he made Rhony the offer? Probably Rhony thought it was a threat, but the more Alfredo considered his comment, maybe he had said it because it was what he secretly wanted, too. But escaping from the ranks of the Shining Path wasn't possible—not from the most violent Communist organization in the world.

The singing had stopped, and suddenly the door of the little church opened, flooding the street with light and then a stream of happy worshipers heading for their humble homes in the streets of Chosica.

"Hey, you guys," whispered Alfredo, "it's over. Rómulo Saúñe will be coming out soon. Stay put till I say to move." This was Alfredo's operation. Their commander had put him in charge as a test of his loyalty: Could he—would he—carry out the order to assassinate Rómulo Saúñe, the evangelical pastor who had so much influence in the surrounding mountain villages?

First one light and then another went off inside

the church, and then two couples came out of the now-darkened doors, closing and locking them behind themselves. The people exchanged hugs, and then one man and woman turned and walked right past the tree with the waiting terrorists, while the other couple went on down the street.

Alfredo and his comrades remained silent until the couple had passed. "Is that him?" whispered Juan. "Let's shoot him now."

"No, that's not them. It's the other couple. Pastor Sauñe and his wife went up the street that way." Alfredo pointed at the receding figures that could barely be seen in the moonlight.

"Oh, so it's *Pastor* Sauñe now, is it?" said Juan. "Sounds like you're rather familiar."

"Well . . . yeah. You know I had to scout out this operation. I've even been to a couple of their meetings. But that's all. Our great leader, Abimael Guzmán, is the only 'pastor' for me."

The three remained under the tree until they saw Rómulo Sauñe and his wife enter a house nearly a block from the church, then they arose, unwrapped the rifles, and moved out. Alfredo carried only his pistol.

"When we get to the door," Alfredo said in an undertone, "you guys hang back and cover me. I'll do the hit." It had been their commander's orders that he be the one to kill the pastor. *"It'll be your way of proving your loyalty after being gone so long,"* he said. Alfredo had agreed. What else could he do?

Clouds drifted across the moon covering the move-

ments of the
three guerrillas.
A dog began bark-
ing, a high yipping
sound. The boys
froze in the shadows. Finally a man cursed at the
dog. The dog yelped, apparently hit by something
the man threw, and then was silent. A door slammed.

After a few moments of silence, the guerrillas continued moving up the street.

Over the door to Rómulo Sauñe's house hung a single light bulb, protected by a shade that looked more like an upside-down pie tin. As Alfredo approached, he considered whether he should knock out the light. He didn't like the idea of standing in front of the door bathed in light. On the other hand, breaking the bulb might attract more attention. He'd be better off leaving the light in place, even if it exposed him for a few moments.

He turned to look at Juan and Rhony. They had dropped back to cover his position as he got closer to the house. Alfredo gave a hand signal for them to stop as he halted just beyond the reach of the light. Everything was silent . . . maybe too quiet. He held his breath until he thought he might faint. Then somewhere in the distance he heard someone's radio or TV playing a commercial for Coca-Cola.

He breathed again.

Taking one last glance at his comrades, Alfredo cocked his pistol, held it upright at shoulder level, and moved into the circle of light.

In three quick steps he was at the house, flattening his back to the wall on the left side of the door. He reached out with his free hand to knock. That's when he saw the cross, hanging on the wall at eye level on the other side of the doorway. Why hadn't he seen it before?

Suddenly he remembered the church in his mountain village of Santa Rosa and the old priest who often carried a small wooden cross—almost like the one hanging beside the door—when he visited the families of Alfredo's village. Alfredo hesitated and frowned. Who was he *really* fighting against here? Wasn't God on the side of the guerrillas? Weren't they struggling against a government that didn't seem to care about the Indians in the mountains? That's what he'd been told. Why did that simple cross make him feel uneasy?

This was no time for doubts. He knocked sharply on the door.

He knocked again and waited a few moments. But there was no answer.

He shifted his pistol to his left hand and thumped the door loudly with the butt of its handle, quickly returning it to his right hand, ready to confront the pastor when he opened the door.

Still there was silence. He looked back at his comrades, wondering what to do.

Then someone spoke from inside. "Yes, who is it?" Ah, it was Sauñe's voice.

"A friend."

"Who?"

"Is the pastor there?"

There was a brief silence on the other side of the door. Then: "No. The pastor isn't here now." Then Alfredo heard footsteps receding from the door.

Forgetting all caution, Alfredo spun around and faced the door head on, pounding on it with his fist. "Señor, wait! Let me in. I must see the pastor." He paused, listening for some hint that his demand would be answered. But no answer came.

Alfredo banged on the door with the barrel of his gun and then stepped back a couple of steps and looked from side to side at the front of the whole house. Surely he had not made a mistake. This was the pastor's house, wasn't it? He had seen him enter it several times. He had seen many other people come to this same door and be admitted by none other than Rómulo Sauñe, the evangelical Indian pastor he was supposed to kill. And just tonight, less than fifteen minutes before, he'd seen him and his wife . . .

"Hey, Juan! Rhony!" he said in a loud whisper. "This is the right door, isn't it? You saw him go in here, didn't you?"

"Yeah, if that was him," answered Rhony. "But we've never seen him before."

It *had* to be the right door. That preacher was just being stubborn. Alfredo stepped back up to the door, quietly this time, and carefully tried the handle. It was locked. He swore, took one step back, and banged again with the barrel of his pistol. Frustrated, he turned away and joined his comrades as they retreated into the shadows.

"We've got to find another way!"

"Let's go around back," said Juan. "There may be another door from the rear."

"Or maybe a window that's not locked," added Rhony.

✧ ✧ ✧ ✧

16

Alfredo and his companions spent the next hour trying to find a way to break into the compound, but all the windows in the thick adobe walls were barred, and the strong gate to a walled garden in the back was locked.

"Why don't we climb over?" suggested Rhony.

"Then what?" Alfredo threw up his hands. "We don't know what room the pastor and his wife sleep in. Even if we could get in, it might be someone else's room."

"So what?" Juan shrugged. "We'd just kill them, too."

"Yeah, and as soon as we started shooting, we'd wake up the whole household. Then we're either facing several people, or Sauñe gets away."

Juan stared at Alfredo in the blue shadows and silver moonlight. Finally he said, "Something doesn't make sense here. We had everything planned, but nothing's working out."

"Yeah," Rhony muttered. "It's like someone's working against us at every turn."

"Then we'll have to go to my backup plan," said Alfredo. He didn't have a backup plan, but his comrades didn't know that. "Let's get some sleep and try again tomorrow."

Chapter 2

Return Visit

The three youthful fighters made their way through the hard-packed dirt streets of Chosica to Juan's aunt's house, where they'd been staying the past few days. The kindly woman had no idea about her nephew's association with the Shining Path or their murderous plans. But as they let themselves in long after midnight, they heard her plaintive voice calling from her bedroom.

"Juan, is that you?"

"Yes, *mi tía*. We're back."

"Oh, good. I was so worried! I wish you wouldn't stay out so late. Nothing good happens after midnight."

"We're fine, *mi tía*. We're fine. You go to sleep now. See you tomorrow."

The boys went to the back room of her small apartment and made themselves as comfortable as possible on the old mattress on the floor. But Alfredo couldn't go to sleep. At first he imagined that the mattress was full of fleas, maybe because a cat often slept on it. But then his mind started replaying the events of the evening.

Why had he failed? How had the hit gone wrong?

Finally, in an attempt to get his mind off the failed attack, he got up and rummaged around in his bag until he found his flute. Then he tiptoed out the back door and climbed the creaking stairs up to the roof of the house. The moon had set, and there were very few lights still on in nearby houses. It was almost as dark and quiet as the lovely nights in his mountains.

Alfredo sat on the edge of a large pot with a tomato plant growing in it, put the flute to his lips, and tried a few breathy notes, but the comforting melodies wouldn't flow. He tapped his foot to create the rhythm of the familiar hand drum and tried to imagine the lilting guitars of the mountain musicians, but he couldn't add his part with the flute.

Something was wrong. Desperately wrong.

Tears fought their way to the surface as Alfredo sat on the roof thinking, possibly for hours, until the eastern sky turned from cobalt to azure to lemon, then gold. What had happened to him? Such a short time ago he had been a carefree boy herding sheep and llamas on the grassy mountain peaks. Then he had no fears. Then he was not trying to kill someone.

Then he could play his flute.

Somewhere a rooster crowed and stirred Alfredo from his thoughts. He descended the old steps as quietly as possible and slipped back into the bedroom. Juan and Rhony were still sleeping. Good. He picked up his bag, dropped in his flute and then his gun, and quietly made his way through the house and out the front door.

Poor farmers were leaving the city to work their faraway fields on the edge of the mountains. Some had a burro or a llama to carry their tools—a shovel, a hoe, a rake—but most carried what they needed on their shoulders. The wealthy hacienda owners in the fertile valleys and rolling foothills didn't live in the dirty town. Besides, they could sleep till the sun was high and let their laborers work their land.

Once the town had come awake and he wouldn't be noticed among the activity of the streets, Alfredo made his way to the church where Rómulo Sauñe had spoken the night before. Just down the street he could see the small house where he and his comrades had intended to attack the preacher. Especially now in the daylight, there was no question that they had been at the right house. But this morning he approached it more out of curiosity than with intent to kill the man inside.

With his sack of belongings over one shoulder, he examined the front of the house. The electric light above the heavy wooden door was now off, but the small cross still hung on the thick adobe wall just to the right. Trying to act casual, Alfredo looked around.

A few kids were playing in the street and an old woman with a dirty red scarf over her head walked away with a distinct limp, but no one seemed to be paying any attention to him.

He took a deep breath and knocked on the door.

Maybe no one would answer again. What would he do if someone did? Maybe he should return to his comrades. Coming back here was a foolish thing to do. And yet—

The door opened, and a man with warm eyes said, "Good morning. Can I help you?" It was the

same voice Alfredo had heard the night before.

Momentarily confused by the man's friendly response, Alfredo said, "Uh . . . is the pastor here?"

"No. The pastor doesn't live here anymore."

"But I've seen you . . . !" Alfredo pointed down the street toward the church.

"Oh, *sí*. I've been filling in for him while I'm in town, but I'm not the pastor of this church. He had to take his wife to the doctor in Ayacucho."

"But you're Rómulo Saúñe, aren't you?"

"Oh, sure. I'm the president of TAWA—a local mission organization that many churches belong to. But"—he stepped back from the doorway and beckoned with his hand—"come in, come in. You look like you could use a cup of coffee."

Alfredo couldn't believe what was happening. He almost tripped over the doorsill as he stepped into the dark entryway.

"Here. Come right in here and have a seat. You want coffee?"

"Uh, *sí*. *Gracias*." Alfredo took in the room he'd been ushered into at a glance. The preacher obviously used it as his study. A small desk sat by the window, and a dilapidated sofa that looked like kids had been jumping on it until the springs broke sat nearby, along with a couple of other chairs. Along one wall was a bookcase with many well-worn books and a few handmade pottery items.

Alfredo stood there with his bag hanging from one hand, not knowing where to sit or what to do, while Rómulo Saúñe disappeared down the hall.

Returning with a steaming mug of coffee in each hand, the preacher said, "*Siéntese,* sit down right there on the soft seat. Here's some coffee. Be careful; it's hot. You want sugar?"

"No. *Gracias.*" Alfredo took his seat on the sofa, letting his bag drop to the dark wooden floor beside him.

"Now," said Rómulo as he pulled up another chair. "What can I do for you so early in the morning?"

Alfredo didn't know what to say. He'd come the night before to kill this man. The gun he had intended to use still sat in the bag beside him. But now he was here because . . . Why *was* he here? It was almost as though someone had compelled him to come. "I—I was here last night. I came to see you after the service, but . . ."

"You weren't at the prayer meeting, were you? I didn't see you there."

"No. No. I came afterward, but you . . . you wouldn't open the door and let me in. It was you, wasn't it, who came to the door and told me that the pastor wasn't here?"

Rómulo Sauñe's eyebrows rose as he tipped his head to the side and allowed his lower lip to stick out. Then he smiled broadly, revealing a set of very white teeth. "*Sí.* I heard you knocking, and I told you that the pastor wasn't here. And, as I've explained, that was technically true. He is in Ayacucho, but . . ." His voice trailed off.

"Why didn't you open the door to see what I wanted?"

"Ah! Well now, that's a different matter. . . . What did you say your name was?"

"Alfredo, Alfredo Garcia." He had no sooner said it than he wished he hadn't told the pastor his last name. That was a sure way to get caught, revealing his last name. But Rómulo continued on as though there had been no interruption.

"The reason I didn't open the door to you last night, Alfredo, may be a curious matter to you. I'm not sure it is something you can understand. In fact, I can't fully explain the reasons myself, but the Holy Spirit of God held me back. Do you know what I'm saying? It was . . . it was as though I could not reach out and unlock the door." He paused and gazed at Alfredo so intently that Alfredo looked away. "I certainly hope you were not in some grave trouble and needed help, but I've learned to obey those gentle leadings from the Holy Spirit. So tell me, why was it you came last night? And why are you here now?"

In answer, Alfredo leaned over and grabbed the bottom of his bag, upending it so that the contents spilled out on the floor—a pair of socks, a plastic bag with stale tortillas, his flute, then—*clunk*—his pistol, and finally a small box of ammunition. Out of the corner of his eye, Alfredo saw Rómulo flinch when the gun hit the floor, but when Alfredo did not reach for it, the preacher seemed to relax again.

"I am a member of the Shining Path," said Alfredo, pointing to his pistol as proof. "Last night I came to assassinate you. It was an order from my commander. He thinks you influence too many mountain people in ways that do not support the revolution." Alfredo looked Rómulo in the eye. "I am still under those orders."

"Then why haven't you shot me?"

Alfredo shrugged and leaned back into the sofa. "I intended to, but—"

Rómulo shook his head. "No. You haven't shot me for the same reason I did not open the door to you last night. You're not fighting against me, Alfredo. You are fighting against God himself, the God of the universe. It is He who would not let me open the door to you last night. And it is He who keeps you from shooting me right now. No one can fight against God and win."

Alfredo began to sweat. Somehow he knew this was true, a truth he had realized without the words to describe it while he sat on the rooftop all night. It was this truth that had compelled him to return to Rómulo's house this morning. His hand shook as he took a sip of coffee, unable now to look the preacher in the eye.

"You know," said Rómulo, "this isn't the first time the Shining Path has tried to kill me and failed."

Alfredo looked up. "Really?"

"Yes, really. My wife and I lived in Ayacucho while I was translating the Bible into our Quechua language—you've seen it, haven't you?"

"Yes, I've seen it." Alfredo *had* seen several people carrying the new Quechua Bible. But he had never read it.

"Well," continued Rómulo, "one day we took a trip

to some distant villages to make sure we were getting the words just right so that everyone could understand it. While we were gone, a whole squad of heavily armed young men attacked our mission station. They fired their machine guns as they crashed through the gate and then began banging on the door of our house, yelling for me to come out." Rómulo smiled. "Of course, I wasn't home. God arranged it that way. So, you see what I mean? You cannot fight God and win, son."

Alfredo wanted to say, *I could kill you now!* But somehow he wasn't so sure, so he just sat in silence. No words would come. Finally Rómulo broke the silence and said, "Tell me, son, how did you get involved with the Shining Path in the first place?"

Did the man really want to hear his story? Alfredo took a deep breath, leaned forward with his forearms resting on his knees, and the words began to come.

Chapter 3

The Assassin's Tale

I was born in the village of Santa Rosa, high in the Andes Mountains. It is the last village on the road. Beyond Santa Rosa there are only trails over the mountain to other villages. We are a poor people, so poor that the government did not think it was necessary to repair our road or set up a school for the children.

When I was younger, there was only one car in our town, an old green Dodge. It had belonged to Señor Morales, but when he died, the men of the village tried to keep it running so we could take crafts down to sell in Ayacucho and return with supplies.

My daily job at that time was to take the sheep and goats up on the mountainsides to find pasture. I took our family animals plus those of three or four other families, and other boys my age did the same, going to other pastures. We also had three llamas, and I would take them, as well, if my father or older brother, Rico, did not need them. The llamas were our most valuable animals. As well as providing wool for weaving cloth, they could carry heavy loads and serve as guards against danger. They were far more intelligent than the sheep.

One day I was herding sheep on the mountain, sitting in my favorite place between two rocks, playing my flute, when the llamas—they always stayed nearby—raised up in alarm. I stood up and looked around but saw no one. I could see the sheep and goats grazing peacefully not too far away. I couldn't see any wild dogs slinking around, and the sky was clear—no thunderstorms coming. So why were the llamas alarmed?

Then suddenly someone started shooting a gun: *blam, blam, blam!* It echoed through the canyons and stampeded the sheep and goats. I frantically looked this way and that—which way had the shots come from?—when three men stepped out from behind some scraggly pine trees. One held a gun pointed up in the air. He fired another shot, and then they all began to laugh.

"Hey, *wayna.* You scared or something?"

"I'm *not* a little boy." I was thirteen at the time.

"Well, if you're so big, then you better take care of your dumb sheep. The people in the village wouldn't want to hear that you let one of them fall into a crevice or over a cliff." They laughed again as I ran off after the frightened sheep.

I had not even crossed the meadow when I heard our llamas trumpeting their frantic *oot . . .hot, oot . . . hot* calls. I turned around just in time to see the bandits dragging them away. The llamas were spitting and kicking and putting up a good fight, but they were no match for the bandits. I didn't know what to do—continue after the sheep or go back and try to rescue our llamas?

In a moment it was too late. The bandits disappeared over the ridge, and since they were grown men with a gun, there wasn't much I could have done, anyway.

This wasn't the first time bandits had stolen from our village. They had become a regular threat, robbing people on the trail, stealing corn and potatoes from our small fields. Sometimes they even came into the village at night and took anything else they wanted.

Our people often asked the government for protection, but the officials did not care about us. They never sent the police or anyone to investigate.

The last straw was when they stole our village car. Of course, there's only one road, and it goes down the mountain, so everyone knew which direction the bandits had gone. Half the village took off after them on foot. Sure enough, about three miles down the mountain, we found our green Dodge, smashed into a huge boulder by the road. Apparently the bandits were going too fast and didn't realize the brakes on our old vehicle didn't work very well.

The men tried to fix the car, but it was hopeless. It's still sitting there today, a rusty hulk beside the road. People have stripped off the tires and taken the engine and anything else of value, but it sits there like a thorn in our foot, a constant reminder of the bandits who were preying on our village.

My father and some other men decided they couldn't let this keep happening. If the government wouldn't protect the village of Santa Rosa, the men of the village would have to do it themselves. They created a posse and went after the bandits. There were only nine of them, and only four had guns—all the guns in the whole village. I'm not sure that any of the guns could even shoot. I know the old shotgun my father took had never been shot that I could remember. And Mama said he didn't have any shells. But I guess they hoped that their numbers would be enough to drive the bandits away.

Three days passed, and then my friend Emilio came running past our house, shouting, "The men are returning! The men are returning!"

The whole village had gathered in the square in front of the little church when the men appeared. They came up the street as a small huddle, holding one another up and moving like a drunken spider. Obviously a couple were wounded, and the Gordillo brothers—the largest and strongest men in town— were carrying a dark roll on their shoulders.

Suddenly the women started wailing and running toward them, with the little children trailing along at their feet. Some of the other boys and I followed, but more cautiously. Even the old priest, holding his small wooden cross high over his head, passed us.

Where was Papa? I could not see him in the small group of men as they approached. I pushed my way through the crowd to get to the men in the center. "Where's Papa? Where's Papa?"

My mother and brother were gathered around the Gordillo brothers, talking frantically. Suddenly Mama's face curled up like a dried apple. She fell to her knees with her hands raised and began to shriek and wail. My brother reached down to hold her shoulders as I pushed toward them.

"Mama! What's wrong? Why are you crying?"

"Papa's dead." Rico spit the words out through gritted teeth. "The Gordillos brought his body back."

For the first time I paid attention to the dark burden that the Gordillos gently laid on the ground. My father. I fell to my knees beside his body, like the breath had been knocked out of me, barely noticing as two or three of the other men, seriously wounded and barely able to walk, were led away with the help of their friends.

That was Saturday, April 4, 1992—the day my father was killed. I'm not sure what happened over the next couple of days. It's all a blur in my mind until after the funeral. I do remember the old priest praying over Papa's open grave behind the church as the whole village stood around. Suddenly I imagined this ridiculous image of that old man himself falling over dead right into the grave with my father. I felt embarrassed. Why would I think of such a crazy vision at a time like that? I have no idea. I guess sometimes a person's mind does strange things.

❖ ❖ ❖ ❖

A few days later, I sat on a rock behind our house trying to play my flute, but very few songs would come. Rico came outside and sat down on the rock beside me. "What are you thinking about?" he asked.

For some reason I told him about imagining the old priest falling into the grave with Papa. "Maybe I had a vision of the future or something."

He snorted. "Some vision! Anyone can predict that that old man won't make it through another winter. What I want in a vision for the future is how we're going to avenge Papa's death."

"Avenge—? What do you mean?"

"Those bandits are still robbing from us. Just yesterday they stole a sack of corn right out of Señora Morales's house. They walked right in and took it! There wasn't a thing she could do. And the government won't even protect us. We gotta do something!"

As the months went by, I thought a lot about what Rico had said. But our mother worried constantly about how we would survive. Mama tried to keep weaving the beautiful blankets she made, but—maybe it was her grief over Papa—she didn't get very much done. With our llamas gone and Papa dead, it fell to my brother and me to work our rocky fields and herd our sheep, patch our roof and gather dried dung for the fire.

Then one day Rico disappeared. I'm five years younger, so I guess he didn't think he had to tell me where he was going or why. And like I said, Mama was too overwhelmed to deal with other things. But I sure felt betrayed, him going off and leaving me with all the work.

Several days later he showed up as unexpectedly as he had disappeared and put twenty *soles,* which is almost six dollars, on the table. It was more money

than Mama could get for three blankets!

"Where'd you get that?" Mama asked, staring at the money. "Where have you been?"

Rico stuck his chin in the air. "I've joined the *Sendero Luminoso,* the Shining Path."

"What?" Mama put her hands on her hips and raised her voice. "What do you know about the Shining Path, anyway? Why haven't you been around here to do your share of the work? How are we going to make it if you go running off?"

"It's the *revolution,* Mama! We're going to avenge Papa's murder and . . . and overthrow the government, too! The bandits steal us blind, while the government does nothing to protect us—or anything else for the common people of Peru, for that matter."

Mama stared at her older son. Then she sighed and knelt on the ground before the fire in our little house. She pushed another piece of llama dung into the flames and looked into the pot that simmered above the fire. Finally she said, "We don't need to avenge your father's death—God rest his soul. Vengeance belongs to God. What we need to do—what *you* need to do—is make yourself useful planting the potatoes."

Rico threw up his hands. "Potatoes, potatoes! We can't just think about potatoes, Mama! Abimael Guzmán was a professor at the university. He understands all about these things, and he knows that the government in Lima only protects the rich and makes them richer while leaving us to the bandits. Has the government ever repaired our roads? Or—or built a school in Santa Rosa so Alfredo can learn to read?"

"I already know how to read," I protested, but Rico ignored me.

"The Shining Path is the official Communist party of Peru." Rico sounded like he was giving a speech. "We are going to take over the country and set up a new government, one that will serve the poor people—the Indians here in the mountains and small villages."

"But Rico, my son! Revolution means war, and war means killing. Bloodshed is never the way, and if you pursue it, you are likely to get killed yourself."

I listened to the two of them argue, but I could see that Rico's mind was set on joining the guerrillas, and nothing else mattered. Mama began to cry. "If you go off fighting, how are we supposed to survive? I can't possibly plant all the potatoes and corn or take care of the house by myself."

"I won't always be away, Mama. This is a peasant army, a people's army. We all have families to take care of. Besides, what about him?" Rico jerked a thumb in my direction. "He's getting big enough to do a lot more than herd sheep. Alfredo,"—my brother turned to me—"it's time you picked up the slack. You'll be the man of the house when I'm gone."

I didn't know what to say. Sure, I liked being called the man of the house, but I'd hoed and planted corn in that rocky soil on the steep mountain field often enough to know that I didn't want to do it by myself, or all the time. What if I didn't get it planted soon enough to catch the rains? What if it all died?

What if it rotted or got eaten by bugs?

"Besides," Rico said, pointing to the twenty *soles* that he had placed on the table, "there's money, too."

"And where does that money come from?" Mama demanded.

"From the Shining Path. We don't get paid, but when there's a need . . ." He paused and then added, "As Comrade Guzmán says, 'From each according to his abilities, to each according to his needs.'"

Mama gave the stew in the pot a fierce stir. "Huh. That little saying is not from your Comrade Guzmán. Karl Marx said it, one of the chief architects of communism."

"How do you know that?" Rico snapped.

"Not every Quechua Indian is ignorant. I do read, you know. That's how I taught the two of you. And I also listen to the radio—I know what the Shining Path is."

Rico lowered his eyes. "I'm sorry, Mama. I didn't mean any disrespect."

Mama stirred the stew in silence for a few moments, then rose to face my brother. "I forgive you, my son. But I am also very worried about you. Communism has never brought the poor people of the world what it promised them. Usually it has brought only suffering and death. And I am afraid that is what it will bring you and me. Listen to me, Rico! I—"

"It's too late, Mother." Rico backed away. "I've . . . I've already joined, and I must go back now."

Chapter 4

Demands of the Revolution

After Rico joined the Shining Path, my brother was often gone for days at a time. He usually came back saying that he had been traveling to other villages, recruiting new members. But one time he started to tell us how he and several comrades had ambushed a government car on the road.

"I don't want to hear about it!" Mama said. "I warned you this would happen—blood-shed and murder."

"Nobody got killed, Mama."

"No thanks to you."

"What do you mean?"

"You call this war—a guer-rilla war!—and you said it was an ambush. Did you have guns?

I take it you didn't just wave down the government car with your hands!" Mama's tone was slightly mocking. "An ambush with guns threatens death. It's only a matter of time until you kill someone. I know what's going on—everyone does. The Shining Path has been killing people all over the country."

Rico's eyes narrowed. "Only traitors."

"Traitors? You mean people who don't do exactly what you say? What kind of freedom is that?"

Rico turned on his heel and walked out the door.

✧ ✧ ✧ ✧

We didn't see Rico again for almost two weeks, and then one day a battered red pickup truck came roaring into Santa Rosa. Half a dozen young men sat in the back or hung to the sides. One of them was Rico.

They stopped in a cloud of dust in the village square. A couple of the guerrillas who had guns began firing them into the air. Soon the whole village gathered to see what was happening. However, when people realized it was the Shining Path, they hung back, making a circle that left the pickup and the guerrillas alone in the center.

One of the men stood up in the back of the truck, while the two with guns positioned themselves on either side of him on the ground. They held rifles at the ready across their chests. The other men, including Rico, marched roughly to the small crowd of onlookers and stood outside our circle with their backs to the people. They stood at parade rest—legs spread, hands clasped behind their back—as if they were there to defend the gathering from outsiders.

I looked around, down the streets, over toward the church, and past various houses. But the Shining Path men were the only outsiders in Santa Rosa that day. Who were they protecting us from?

The man standing in the back of the truck wore a camouflage army jacket and a matching cap. He raised one hand for silence—though no one was talking. In his other hand he held a bullhorn, a loudspeaker that squealed and squawked as he shouted into it so everyone could hear. "Welcome, people of Santa Rosa. I am Comrade Albino, commander of your local Shining Path warriors."

I couldn't help wondering why he was welcoming us, as though this was his village and we were the visitors. But he continued to give a speech about how all the people needed to join together to resist the corrupt government in Lima. He listed all the ways the government had neglected the mountain villages, and that was certainly true. We all knew that from experience. We never saw anyone from the government except when they wanted to collect taxes or to tell us we couldn't do something like build a dam across our stream.

By this time our old Catholic priest had made his way from the church to the square and was straining to see over some of the taller people to see what was happening.

Comrade Albino told us how army troops had

attacked some of the Shining Path fighters who were defending their village. He boasted about how they had defeated the government soldiers and driven them away.

Originally Rico had said he had joined the Shining Path to avenge our father's death by hunting down the bandits. I listened carefully to the commander, but I didn't hear him say anything about fighting bandits. All he talked about was fighting the government. It made me wonder what had happened to Rico's goals. Maybe Mama was right: Vengeance should be left to God, or it would get all confused and hurt other people.

When Commander Albino finished his speech, he asked how many villagers would pledge themselves to support the Shining Path. No one responded. I think we all shrank back, not wanting to get involved in something we either didn't understand or thought might be wrong.

The Shining Path leader called out to the priest, who was still standing at the back of the circle. "How about you, Father? Are you with us or against us?"

The old man just ducked his head and ignored the question.

"Bring our fine priest right on up here," said Commander Albino.

Two of the "guards" quickly walked over and grabbed the old man by his arms. The people stepped back to leave an opening in their circle for the guerrillas to push the priest toward the truck.

"I could not hear you back there, Father. But I

can see you are a leader in this commu-
nity, so I'm sure the people will follow your
example. Tell us loud and clear so everyone
can hear: Are you with us or against us?"

I could not hear what the priest mumbled for an
answer, but others who were closer later said that he
answered, "I am for God only."

"What sorry peasants you people of Santa Rosa

are if that is your leader!" yelled Commander Albino. "You need a new leader, someone who is in tune with the future. Let the past bury the past!"

He turned to the two guards who were holding the old priest. "Lock him in his church. Let it be his tomb. He's not worth remembering anymore."

The guards roughly pushed the priest toward the church, slapping him on the back of the head so hard that he almost fell to the ground with every blow. At the church they threw him through the doors, and I heard him cry out in pain as he hit the floor. Then they closed the doors and chained and locked the handles together. I have no idea where they got that chain and lock; it wasn't on the door before.

I think we were all shocked by how rough the guerrillas had been with a priest. Most people give God's servants a little bit of honor, even if they don't go to church very often. I was staring at the church door and the two men walking back from it when I recognized the voice of my brother yelling through the bullhorn.

I turned around and saw that Rico had climbed up into the bed of the pickup. He smiled and spread out one arm, as though he wanted to embrace everyone. "Friends, neighbors, comrades, you all know me. I am Comrade Rico Garcia. I'm from this village. I grew up here. That's why I know you will trust me and do what I say.

"As our valiant commander has said, we are fighting our true enemy—your enemy and my enemy—the national government that cheats us through high taxes without giving us any services. But what is worse, they have now turned against us. They have targeted us. We are here to protect you, but the government wants to kill us. The army has driven us into hiding and pursues us mercilessly through the mountains. But it can never win, because we are the people. We are you, and we know that you will support us."

I'd never heard my brother give a speech. In fact, he was usually the quiet one when the townsmen and boys stood around telling stories in the evening. Now he sounded like he was arguing with Mama, but he was talking to the whole village.

"What I want you to do," he continued, "is show your loyalty, show your appreciation for our sacrifice by supporting us. Now, here's what we are going to do. We will return next Saturday afternoon, and at that time you will be given the opportunity to demonstrate your support for the Shining Path—your own revolutionary liberators—by making donations of corn and potatoes and beans. Bring us coats and warm clothes so we can keep warm in the caves and huts in which we've been forced to live."

At that moment Commander Albino grabbed the bullhorn away from Rico. The loudspeaker squealed loudly as he put it up to his lips. "Yes, and bring us gasoline and money. And above all, bring us your guns so that we may defend you."

"We don't have any guns," shouted one of the Gordillo brothers.

"Now, you know that's not true," said the

commander, as though he were talking to a child. "I happen to know you took some guns with you when you went to find those bandits you've been complaining about."

"Huh!" snorted Andrés Gordillo, the younger of the two brothers. "Three old guns, and two of them wouldn't shoot."

"Then you only need to contribute that third gun," said the commander, his voice still sticky sweet. "I will be looking for it on Saturday. In fact, I will be looking for *you!*" He pointed at Gordillo. "You would be wise to make arrangements to join us. A big strong man like you could be very useful in our struggle." Gordillo stepped back.

"And money!" shouted the commander, addressing everyone again. "Don't forget to bring money. We will see if Comrade Rico's village is as loyal as he said you would be."

With that, the other guerrillas climbed into the pickup. The engine roared to life, and they drove off in another cloud of dust.

I started to wave at my brother, but he wasn't looking my way. And then I realized that some of my neighbors from Santa Rosa were frowning at me. It had been kind of exciting for my brother to return with the Shining Path and make a speech to the village, but I hadn't taken into account that some of them might dislike the Shining Path.

Suddenly someone said, "The priest. We must get him out of the church."

Like a herd of llamas, the whole crowd ran over to

the church. At first people worked at getting the door open. The Gordillos pulled on the door, but the chain was too strong. There weren't any other doors, so I ran around to the side and got someone to boost me up and through the window.

The inside of the church seemed dark until my eyes adjusted. "Father, are you okay?" I called softly. But there was no answer.

Finally I found the old man sprawled on the floor with his neck at a crooked angle and his head against a bench.

"Father? Wake up! You gotta get up." But he didn't move.

I went to the door and banged on it from the inside. "Help, somebody! You gotta get in here," I yelled. "I think he's hurt."

I could hear people working outside, straining and pulling on the door. Then there was a ripping sound, and the doors swung open, the bright light flooding in. Someone had found an iron pipe that they used as a pry bar to rip the handle off the doors that were chained together.

The people pushed past me and huddled around the body of the priest. Carefully they picked up the old man and carried him out of the church and over to Señora Morales's house, the one nearest the church. Would our priest die? Had the Shining Path killed him?

I went home thinking about the vision of him falling into the grave with my father. Would he be the next person from the village to die?

Chapter 5

The Shining Path of Jesus

To our great relief, the old priest suffered only a knock on the head and was soon walking around town as usual, except with a lump and red scar as testimony of his recent "battle wounds."

All that week the people of Santa Rosa asked each other what they were going to do about the requested "gifts." Would they support the Shining Path? Or would they defy the guerrillas' demands?

As the village men and older boys sat around in front of *El Mercado Bueno*—our combined grocery store, gas pump, and post office—Andrés Gordillo chugged half a bottle of Coca-Cola and wiped his mouth with the back of his hand. "Huh!

The Shining Path is nothing but a gang of thieves, robbing us poor people while telling us that they are our defenders. They keep telling us how much they care about poor people, but they haven't done one thing to make our life better, and now they want *us* to give to them? Not likely!"

"You'd better be careful what you say," said his older brother. "Remember what that guerrilla commander said about you."

"I don't care what he said. There's no way I'm going to fight for those crooks. And I'm not going to contribute anything for them, either."

"Do what you please," murmured his brother. "Just keep it quiet." He glanced at me as though he thought I was going to report his brother to the Shining Path.

Andrés pushed his hat back on his head and scowled. "Well, you can keep quiet if you want to, but *I* don't think *any* of us ought to keep quiet. I think we ought to all join together and resist them. What could they do to us if the whole village refused to cooperate? You mark my word. If we give them anything next Saturday, they'll just be back for more the following week. Never give in to extortion is what I say. These Shining Path thugs are no better than the bandits before them."

Several other villagers nodded, and the priest who had just joined the group put his hand up to the wound on his head. "That's true. No better than bandits."

But I was troubled. Several people seemed to look

at me to see how I would respond. I didn't have anything to say, but for the first time I realized that people were assuming that because "Comrade Rico" was my brother, I might be a threat to them. When I had seen Rico standing in the back of that truck talking to the people of Santa Rosa, I felt proud of him. He seemed important. But now I wasn't so sure Rico was a hero.

I stepped away and slipped around the corner of the store.

Surely Rico hadn't become a bandit like the men who had killed our father! Hadn't he started out determined to avenge our father's death?

✧ ✧ ✧ ✧

But when Saturday arrived, instead of the old red pickup filled with guerrillas shooting their guns into the air, a Chevy station wagon pulled into town with three Quechua men and one woman. When they got out of their car, they greeted us and said they were missionaries and had come to preach about Jesus Christ.

"You have a priest for your church here, don't you?" said one of the men. "Is he around? We would like to talk to him about showing *The Jesus Film* to the whole village."

"Well, yeah, we have a priest," I said, eager to see a movie.

"Ha! We're lucky we still *have* a priest. The Shining Path almost killed him."

I turned around. It was my mother who had offered this bit of news to the strangers. She was dressed in her blue dress with the heavy wool red jacket over it, beautifully embroidered in black and green. Her round-topped black hat was pulled low on her forehead, and her mouth was turned down in a hard frown.

Behind her, leaning on a walking stick on the top of which he had tied the small cross he carried everywhere, was our village priest, squinting his eyes and studying the newcomers.

"We are sorry to hear that. I hope you are recovering, Father." The visitor stepped forward and shook the priest's hand. "I'm Rómulo Sauñe, and I come from Chakiqpampa, not far away . . . just over those mountains a few miles." He pointed over his shoulder. "I was one of the people who helped translate the Bible into the Quechua language. Maybe you have heard about that?"

"Yes. Oh, yes!" Joy transformed the old man's wrinkled face. "I bought a copy when I was in Ayacucho four years ago. But I can only read Spanish . . . and a little Latin. As you can tell from my speech, even when I speak Quechua, it is with an accent as thick as a storm cloud. But if I had more Bibles, I could give them to the people."

"I think we can arrange that." Rómulo Sauñe smiled. "I have a few copies in my car. But I'd also like to know if we could show the village a movie about Jesus Christ"—he glanced around the square—"maybe over there on the side of the church where the wall is flat, we could pin up a white sheet?"

"About Jesus Christ? Yes, yes. We would love to see it, wouldn't we?" The priest nodded to the villagers standing around. Everyone nodded back. A film? This was exciting.

"However, we have one problem," my mother pointed out. "We don't have any electricity in Santa Rosa."

"No problem." Rómulo Sauñe grinned broadly. "We brought our own generator. We'll set it up. You tell everyone to be here by the time it gets dark, and we'll show the movie about the life of Jesus Christ!"

By then we'd all forgotten that the Shining Path was supposed to come to town that day and collect our contributions. Some of the villagers had seen movies in Ayacucho. Others had only heard about pictures that moved and talked just like real people. But the excitement rose all through the afternoon.

✧ ✧ ✧ ✧

By the time the sun had gone to bed behind the mountains, I think everyone in the village had gathered alongside the church to see the movie. Even some Indians who lived out of town in houses higher up in the mountains had heard about it and came down. A large crowd gathered, maybe sixty people or more.

The children sat on the ground, and those of us who were older stood behind them. The priest and a few of the older people—like my mother—brought

chairs to sit on. I squeezed in on the side of the crowd where I could get a good view of the sheet.

One of the visitors cranked the generator, Rómulo Sauñe flipped a switch, and the movie flickered to life.

I'd only seen two movies in my whole life. They were about big cities and fast cars from Hollywood. But right from the beginning, I could tell that this movie was about poor people like us. In fact, they lived in a land that seemed very similar to our mountains. The villages were small, with houses made of stone and mud bricks, with dirt floors.

Some of the houses in Santa Rosa have tin roofs, but several are like the houses in the movie, with grass or occasionally tile roofs. The land was dry and dusty, and people either walked or rode horses or donkeys.

I think we all cried when the Roman soldiers nailed Jesus to the cross. Even the Gordillo brothers were wiping their sleeves across their eyes. It seemed so cruel and unfair that someone who was so kind and loving should have to die when he hadn't done anything wrong.

When the movie was finished, Rómulo Sauñe explained that because Jesus was God's Son, his death paid the penalty for our sins, so we could be forgiven . . . if we asked God to forgive us "in Jesus' name." He explained that meant, "because Jesus had paid our penalty."

Then Rómulo Sauñe said, "If you are sorry for the wrong things you have done and want to stop doing them, then ask God to forgive you in Jesus' name. If you want to give your life to Christ and live for Him, raise your hand."

It seemed like everyone was raising their hand. I started to do the same, because I knew that I had done a lot of wrong things, and I wanted God to forgive me, too.

"Alfredo, Alfredo!" A low voice called my name from the dark.

I tried not to pay attention—I wanted to hear what Rómulo Sauñe was saying—but the call became more insistent, and I realized it was my brother, Rico. "What do you want?" I whispered into the darkness.

"Come here. I need to talk to you!"

"Not now!"

"Yes, now! You better get over here if you know

what's good for you." When I didn't budge after a few moments, he added, "You care about Mama, don't you?"

I turned. Of course I cared about Mama. What in the world did he mean by that? Was Mama in some kind of danger?

"Then you better get over here right now!"

I slipped away from the crowd and followed my brother around to the back of the church where the cemetery was. We stopped not far from Papa's grave, and Rico gave my sleeve a yank, turning me around to face him. "What is that all about? What's going on over there?"

"That? It was a movie about Jesus. It was great. You should have seen it."

"I did see most of it, but I couldn't hear. We were over on the other side of the square. Everyone was looking at the movie and didn't see us come into town. But Comrade Albino says that Jesus stuff is no good. He says it gets people's minds off the revolution."

"So what? What good has the revolution ever done for us, anyway?" I remembered what Andrés Gordillo had said, and since I was already mad at my brother for dragging me away from the movie, I asked the question just to get back at him.

"What has the revolution done? How could you possibly ask such a thing! You better watch your mouth, Alfredo. That kind of talk could get you in a lot of trouble, and there wouldn't be anything I could do to help you, either. Now, you listen to me." He grabbed my arms and gave me a shake. "You tell everyone in town that we'll be back next Saturday, and they had better have their gifts ready for us by then. Or else!"

I jerked out of his grip. "Or else what? Hey—"

But Rico had disappeared into the night.

"Wait a minute!" I called softly after him. "What did you mean about Mama? You said I'd better come with you if I cared about her. What was that all about?"

But Rico was gone.

Chapter 6

Betrayal

All that week the only thing people talked about was Jesus—Jesus this and Jesus that. Our old priest was the most excited of all about all the members of his flock who had found new faith after watching *The Jesus Film*. He often sat on the bench in front of *El Mercado Bueno* and talked to the villagers who came to the store. "This is good! This is the way it should always be. People should put Jesus first. I just didn't know how to preach very well in the Quechua language so that you could understand."

"Oh, Father," my mother protested. "You have always been a good priest to us. You have pastored the people of Santa Rosa very well."

The old priest shook his head. "That's another matter. I am old, and when I die the bishop has said he will not be able to replace me. There's just not enough money. Santa Rosa will not have a priest, but all of you need a pastor, especially now that you have given your lives to following Jesus. This must become a strong church, a church that is known among all the villages of these mountains."

"Santa Rosa?" boomed Andrés Gordillo, who had just walked up. "Why would anyone want to know about Santa Rosa? We are just the last stop on an old road full of ruts and chuckholes."

"Yes, yes, but with God, all things are possible," said our priest. "I spoke to Rómulo Saūñe when he was here. He said that a man has been attending his Bible institute in Ayacucho. He's Quechua and a good man who has said he would be willing to come and be the pastor here in Santa Rosa."

We stared at each other in silence. A new pastor for Santa Rosa, an Indian like ourselves?

Finally my mother said, "But would he be a priest?"

"No, but Pastor Jorge could teach you the Bible. He could build a strong church."

"But what will we do for a priest?"

The old man shrugged. "Maybe the bishop would send a visiting priest from time to time. In the meantime, you'll have God's Word in the Quechua language and someone to teach it to you. I have several more of those new Bibles now. Rómulo Saūñe left them with me. We will use them on Sunday."

My mother tossed her head. "Why not during the week?"

The old priest chuckled. "Indeed, why not? But everyone will have to promise to take good care of them."

❖ ❖ ❖ ❖

The idea of someone new—especially a pastor— moving to Santa Rosa to live with us was very unusual. During my whole life, the only people I'd ever known to move to our village was a family who had lived higher in the mountains. The father died, and the family moved into town to live with the grandparents. Otherwise no one new had ever come to Santa Rosa. People left the village to get jobs in Ayacucho or other cities sometimes, but no one ever moved here.

But I had more immediate things to worry about. The Shining Path was coming back on Saturday, and I was supposed to tell everyone to have their gifts ready.

"Mama," I asked that evening as we ate our boiled potatoes, "what do you think we should contribute to the Shining Path?"

"Nothing!" she snarled. Her face displayed a dark frown as she rocked back and forth and turned to put a stick into the fire.

"Nothing?" I nearly choked on my potatoes. "But we can't do that! Rico warned me that the whole town had better have their gifts ready, 'or else!'"

"Or else, what?"

"That's what I asked, but he left without answering." I thought for a few moments. "But earlier he said something else. When I didn't come with him right away to talk like he wanted me to, he said I'd better come if I knew what was good for me. Then he added, 'You care about Mama, don't you?' as though something bad might happen to you if I didn't come with him. What did he mean, Mama? I don't want anything bad to happen to you."

"Ah!" She waved her hand. "He doesn't know what he's talking about. That's what I meant about all this revolution stuff. It leads only to fear. I am not going to be threatened, especially not by my own son. Let the Shining Path collect their 'contributions' from other people, but I've got nothing to offer."

I understood what my mother was saying. I felt pretty much the same. But I could not dismiss Rico's warning so easily. In the days that followed I reminded everyone that the Shining Path was coming back on Saturday and that they'd better have their gifts ready.

"We don't care about the Shining Path," said one woman at the store. Then she added, "Do you know what the real shining path is? It was that light that made the moving picture on the church last Saturday night. Did you notice how that was like a path of light?" Others in the store nodded. "Well, that was the real shining path. It's what showed us the way to live!" Everyone cheered, but I sank into silence.

Soon they were again talking about Jesus and

the possibility that a new pastor would come to Santa Rosa.

I walked away. It seemed hopeless, but at least *I* would be ready when the Shining Path returned. I worked two afternoons that week rebuilding the rock wall on the south side of the Gordillos' house where their donkey had gone crazy and kicked it down. They paid me with two fat hens.

✧ ✧ ✧ ✧

When the old pickup with the Shining Path soldiers rolled into the village square the next Saturday afternoon, I had my contribution ready. I held the chickens upside down by their feet, one in each hand.

The guerrillas began firing their weapons into the air to announce their arrival. One even had an automatic AK-47 assault rifle that buzzed through its bullets with an ear-splitting racket as small children scrambled to pick up the hot shell casings. Slowly the sullen villagers began to gather, some carrying small bags of food, some old clothes.

"Is that all you brought?" yelled the man with the automatic weapon. He grabbed an armload of old clothes from a frightened Señora Morales and threw them in a heap on the ground, then began firing into them with his gun. "You had better bring us good clothes, clothes that are worthy of the revolution," he yelled, "or that will be your fate!" And he squeezed off another burst of gunfire.

59

Everyone shrank back in fright, and then my brother yelled, "Alfredo, come here!"

I was so scared that I almost ran away, but Rico picked up his bullhorn. His voice squawked through its tinny amplifier. "Look, everyone! My brother is only a boy, but he has brought two fat chickens. What's the matter with the rest of you? Bring us gifts worthy of the revolution, gifts worthy of paying for your freedom. Don't forget that we are fighting for you!"

I stepped forward beside my brother who stood near the truck, and he grabbed the chickens and raised them in the air for everyone to see.

Suddenly one of the chickens seemed to explode, sending feathers everywhere; an instant later we heard a rifle shot. Then more gunfire seemed to be coming from several directions.

"It's an ambush!" yelled Commander Albino.

The villagers screamed and began running for cover or falling flat on the ground, hoping not to be hit. Dust was flying everywhere. The guerrilla with the AK-47 jumped into the back of the pickup and began firing, first one direction and then another. It was obvious he didn't know where he was aiming.

Letting the remaining unharmed but wildly squawking chicken fly away, Rico grabbed me and threw me into the back of the pickup and then dove in behind me to lie flat on the floor, partially protected by the sides of the truck. The truck's engine roared to life, and the tires began spitting gravel as the truck spun around in a U-turn and headed out of town. The two guerrillas hanging on the running

boards fired their weapons
as fast as they could.

The last thing I saw as we headed out of the
village was our old priest coming out of the doors of
the church with both hands held high, as though he
were signaling for the shooting to stop. A long burst

of gunfire rattled over my head as the guerrilla with the AK-47 sprayed the village again, and then I saw our priest suddenly stop, hunch forward, and fall to the ground.

"Our priest!" I screamed. "You shot our priest!"

Rico ignored me. But when we were out of range and the shooting had stopped, he yelled toward the front of the truck, "What was that all about?"

In the cab, Commander Albino twisted his head and yelled through the broken-out back window of the pickup. "It was an ambush! Didn't you see their uniforms? An *army* ambush. Someone in that stinking little village betrayed us to the army."

Rico sat up in the back of the truck, an angry scowl on his face. "Somebody betrayed us? But who?"

"*Guess* who," snarled the man with the AK-47 as he slammed home a fresh banana clip of bullets. "But it won't happen again!"

"Our *priest*?" I couldn't believe it. "You killed our priest because you thought he informed the army?"

"Well, I sure hope it wasn't you, kid." The man laughed. "But what's one old priest more or less? He should have stayed in that church where we threw him the last time we were in town."

All I could think about as Rico and I bounced along in the back of that old pickup was the vision I'd had of the priest falling into our father's grave. One violent death. Now two. It wasn't the winter that had taken the old man's life.

Now what would become of my little town?

Chapter 7

What Happens to Deserters

The Shining Path hideout was nothing like I had imagined. It was just some old Inca ruins with a makeshift corrugated tin roof. There were no beds or bunks. The nineteen men slept where they could on the dirt floor or out under the stars.

"So, who'd you bring back with you?" asked the commander.

Rico grinned. "Comrade Albino, this is my brother, Alfredo."

The commander took off his camouflage cap and wiped his forehead as he looked me up and down. "He's pretty young."

"Yes, but he is the one who brought us the chickens."

"Chickens? I don't see any

chickens. Who needs chickens? Don't you understand? This revolution isn't about gathering chickens! It's about winning the hearts and minds of the people. Somebody in that village betrayed us and almost got us killed, and all you can think of is a couple of chickens. I want to know who betrayed us. That person's going to pay!"—by this time he was shouting—"And, if we don't find that person, we will start with the oldest to the youngest, and everyone will pay!"

Comrade Albino sneered at me. "Make yourself useful, kid. Go fetch some water! No one gets a free ride in this man's army!" He turned on his heel and marched away.

"The buckets are over there," whispered Rico. "The closest water is a tiny stream at the bottom of that steep ravine over there. Go get it."

I shuffled over to the buckets and picked up a couple. I hadn't asked to come here, and I didn't like being bossed around like a servant.

"If you want to keep on Comrade Albino's good side, you better show a little hustle, boy," said one of the guerrillas.

I scowled at him. What did I care about Comrade Albino's "good side"? But he answered my question without me saying anything. "It could keep you alive."

I moved a little faster and headed off down the trail toward the ravine Rico had pointed out. From the camp, the slope of the land looked like the ravine was no more than thirty yards away, but the farther

I walked over the rounded brow of the hill, the farther away the real ravine was.

Once I got to the steep ravine, I was able to climb down into it by holding the empty buckets in one hand and using my other hand to hold on to the rocks. But once the pails were full of clear, cold water, I could carry only one at a time while climbing out.

I had gone back down for the second bucket when I heard some shots being fired up in the camp. At first I thought the army had followed us back to the Shining Path camp and was attacking the rebels, but the firing stopped after only a few shots. Still, I approached cautiously, not knowing what might have happened. Several guerrillas were moving about the camp, so I decided it must be safe. The buckets were so heavy I staggered like a drunken man whenever I stepped on an uneven spot in the trail.

"Hey, boy, set those buckets over there by the mess tent," barked Comrade Albino. "Then go up by that tree line"—he pointed up the hill—"and dig a grave. Make the hole at least as deep as you are tall."

What? A grave? The vision of the old priest falling into my father's grave flashed in my mind. Was he going to force me to dig my own grave and then dump me in it after shooting me? He must have mistaken the frightened look on my face for not understanding where to dig, because all he said was, "You can't miss the spot. There are a couple of other graves there already and a pick and shovel around somewhere. Now move it."

The earlier warning of the guy who told me that being quick might keep me on Comrade Albino's "good side" was reason enough to get me moving this time. I found the pick and shovel and headed toward the trees, all the time trying to spot Rico. Was my life in danger? What should I do if it was? But I didn't see him or anyone else I felt I could trust with my question.

The ground was hard and rocky, and roots from the nearby trees made the digging exceptionally difficult. I thought about running away, but where could I go? This was Shining Path territory, and I had no idea whether there were any friendly villages around or how to get to them. As I dug, I glanced at the camp below to make sure no one was watching me. Then I'd look into the nearby trees. Was there a trail in there somewhere that I could follow? Where would it lead?

The shadows on the hillside were long when one of the guerrillas came wandering up my way. He carried his gun slung over his shoulder. He wasn't approaching with very much purpose in his step. But that gun made me nervous. Could he be my executioner?

The hole was almost up to my waist. I dug faster.

"That's not long enough."

I looked up and had to shade my eyes from the setting sun silhouetting the soldier. He didn't look any older than Rico. "I know. The commander said to make it as deep as I am tall. I'm getting there."

"Yeah, but it isn't long enough, either." He pointed at first one end and then the other. "It's no longer than you are tall, and this guy was as tall as I am."

I looked up at him again. From my position down in the hole, he did look pretty tall. Wait a minute— he said *this guy* was as tall as he was. *This guy* must be someone else! I got brave. "Who was he?"

"A deserter. Don't know his name. He ran off before I joined the Shining Path. They only caught him this morning, but I had to be part of the firing squad."

My mouth went dry. "You killed him?"

He snorted nervously. "Hope not. There were six of us in the firing squad. One person's rifle had a blank in it. Maybe that was me and I didn't shoot him."

I leaned on my shovel and squinted up at him.

"One out of six? Chances are, you did, though, huh?"

"Well . . ." He looked around as though he was concerned that someone else might overhear him, then crouched down beside the hole I was digging. "Actually, I aimed to the side. I don't like killing. But if you tell anyone, I'll shoot you."

So why did he tell me? I didn't want to know. I went back to throwing shovelfuls of dirt out of the hole. My visitor stood up. "Like I said, you better make that hole longer, and hurry up about it, too." He disappeared into the shadows.

It was completely dark with only the stars for light when I decided I was finished, hoping the hole was deep and long enough.

My stomach pinched with hunger, and I was so tired I could hardly climb out of the hole. I could taste grit in my dry mouth—I was probably covered with dirt. Exhausted, I sat down on the mound of dirt I'd made and stared down the hill at the camp. The glow from a couple of fires lighted the buildings and the men as they moved around. There was probably food, if I had the energy to walk down and get it, but all I did was sit there, feeling alone and confused. How in the world did I end up here? My brother was one of the guerrillas! Was I one of their prisoners?

I pulled my flute out of my pocket and knocked it against my hand to dislodge any dirt that had collected in it. I put it to my lips and blew a few tentative notes. Finally the notes came clearly, and I played a few songs. Somehow they carried my mind away to more pleasant places, carefree times on the mountains herding the sheep or dancing at a holiday celebration in the village. I looked up at the stars and wondered whether God was watching. Did He care what was happening to our village? It was such a small village with nothing but poor Indians.

I had started another song when Rico spoke to me from the dark. "Hey, Alfredo. Want something to eat? Better come on down."

❖ ❖ ❖ ❖

The next morning my muscles still ached from all that digging. As I sat on an old truck tire eating a tortilla, two of the guerrillas walked by. "You. Come with us, and bring that shovel you were using yesterday."

They went around the corner of a building, picked up a long item rolled in some old blankets, and lifted the load onto their shoulders. It took me a moment to realize it must be the body of the man who had been executed the day before.

The men headed off up the trail toward the trees. I started to follow and then stopped. I didn't want to be close to a dead body. What did they need me for, anyway?

"Come on!" one called. "And get that shovel."

I looked around, trying to think of some place I could hide. The shovel was already up there. They didn't need me. But Commander Albino was leaning in the open doorway of one of the buildings, watching me. He reached into the pocket of his camouflage jacket and pulled out a pack of cigarettes. He lit one, letting the smoke curl up over his face, causing his eyes to squint as he stared right at me.

Without further hesitation, I turned and followed the men up the hill.

At the grave, the men simply slid the body off their shoulders and let it drop with a loud thud into the hole I'd dug. They both looked in for a moment. "Too bad," one said, then they started back down the path.

I had been a short distance behind them, but I stepped aside as they passed. The talkative one punched me in the chest with his finger—it hurt. "You fill it in!" The other one chuckled as they left.

I walked to the hole and peeked in. The blanket roll lay at the bottom, looking somehow like a body and yet not like a body—it could have been anything rolled up in those old blankets. I had a sudden urge to pull away the blankets and see the man's face. I wanted to know what he looked like. Was he as mean looking as Commander Albino or as harmless as my father? Was he as young as Rico or as old as our old priest? Who was he? Why had he deserted? Maybe he just didn't want to be there—like me.

But I'd have to get in that hole to pull back the blanket, and the thought sent chills down my spine. I grabbed the shovel sticking out of the mound, plunged it in, and threw in the first load. The dirt thudded in the bottom just like the body had. I swallowed the lump in my throat. It didn't seem right, dropping rocks and clods of dirt on that poor man, almost like I was stoning him. The next shovel load I lowered carefully and let it spill softly over the wrapped feet. I covered his legs and body with those that followed, but somehow I couldn't dump the dirt on where his head was.

It was just a job that had to be done, I told myself. Everyone dies and has to be buried; someone has to do it. But, my mind argued as I kept putting loads of dirt on his lower body, the Shining Path had shot this man. They had also shot our priest, and he was probably being buried today, too. In my mind's eye I could see the little graveyard back in my town of Santa Rosa. Would our priest's grave be near my father's? Would the whole village be there to show him honor?

Tears clouded my eyes and I blinked them away. When I looked into the hole, the dirt from the end where I had been dumping it had slid to the other end and covered the man's head. I could no longer see the blanket. That made my job easier, and I began scooping the remaining dirt into the hole faster, until the grave was full and mounded up. Finally my awful job was done.

When I finished, I made a crude cross from a couple of sticks tied together with long strands of grass and stuck it into the ground at the head of the grave. I thought someone ought to pray, but I didn't even know the man's name, so I played my flute. The notes escaped into the thin mountain air, but they brought a little comfort—something I needed desperately.

Because it felt like everything in my world had gone crazy.

Chapter 8

Inside Protection

The days with the Shining Path stretched into weeks, during which I was required to do the most unpleasant work in the camp—chopping wood, lugging water, and cleaning out the stinking latrines. Every couple of days the guerrillas headed out of camp "to advance the revolution."

"How come I've got to stay here and wash all the pots and pans?" I complained to Rico one morning as the rest of the men were preparing to leave. "They pick on me all the time, making me do the dirty work!"

"*Shh!*" he hissed. "Nobody's picking on you." He looked around as though concerned someone might overhear us. "*I'm* the one who keeps volunteering you for camp duty. I'm your inside protector."

"You what? Why? I get bored hanging around here, and look at my hands. They're shriveled up like prunes from washing stuff all the time."

"But you're safe here." He glanced around uneasily. "I don't want you to get shot or captured by the army. At least you're safe here. Now quit complaining."

But that evening when I heard where they'd gone, I felt even more left out.

"Guess where we went today?" Rico said, flopping down on his sleeping mat after returning with the other soldiers. "Santa Rosa."

I looked up from shining the commander's boots. "Did you see Mama?"

"No. We were too busy teaching indoctrination classes. Santa Rosa isn't very cooperative—Comrade Albino says it's because of the Christians."

"Christians? Isn't everyone Christian?"

"Not us. Not the people's army." His tone was boastful. "The rich want the poor to believe in God so we'll endure our suffering while we patiently wait for heaven. But we want our share now, right here on earth. The 'hereafter' is just a fairy tale. And we don't believe in God, either."

"But, Rico, you were baptized!"

"Huh! Of course I was baptized. Everyone was baptized as a baby, but that doesn't mean anything to me now. Besides, it is these evangelicals who are causing problems in the villages. They won't come to our meetings, and they tell people they should follow God rather than us." Rico wiped his sleeve across his dirty forehead. "Since the old priest died, there's a new man in Santa Rosa. They call him Pastor Jorge."

Died? Was killed, you mean, I thought. But I remembered that the old priest had told us Rómulo Sauñe had trained a pastor who might come to Santa Rosa.

"This so-called pastor—he's not even a priest!—says that God cured him from an illness, so he will always serve the Lord and never submit to the Shining Path." Rico spit on the floor. "How foolish! We're going to show him."

I remembered images from *The Jesus Film* flickering on the white sheet hanging on the side of the adobe church, showing scenes of Jesus Christ healing the crippled, the sick, and the blind. I shrugged. "I suppose I'd serve Him, too."

"What? What are you talking about?"

"Well, if I was sick and Jesus healed me, I'd probably serve Him. Why not?"

"Why not? Because this Jorge guy is making it all up. He says that at night God speaks to him and says things like, 'Son, how are you?' or 'I've got an important mission for you.' Ha. The Shining Path has the only important mission for Peru."

I picked up the commander's other boot and began brushing off the dirt, avoiding Rico's eyes. Was this my brother talking like this? I felt like I didn't even know him anymore.

"When this new pastor hears what happened to

the church over in Huanta," said Rico sourly, "he'll soon change his mind—that is, if he cares more for his people than for his Jesus stories."

There was something strange about Rico's voice. I stopped putting polish on the boot and watched him out of the corner of my eye.

"What are you looking at?"

I shrugged. "Thought you were going to tell me what happened in Huanta."

"Huh. You don't want to know." But he couldn't help boasting. "All right, I'll tell you. We had warned the people several times to quit praying and come out of their church to listen to us. But they wouldn't obey. So . . . so we torched the church."

I dropped the boot and stared at him.

Rico saw my look. "Well, the pastor there was stubborn, too. It was just an old wooden building with a thatch roof—went up in flames in a couple of minutes. Several people were killed in the fire, and many more were hurt trying to get out, but that pastor . . . he walked out the front door of the church, holding his own son in his arms. The roof was gone and half the walls had caved in, but he yelled at us, 'We serve the living God! We will not serve two masters! We will not serve the Shining Path!' And then—can you believe this?—he pointed his finger right at me and said, 'You are in the hands of the devil.' Oh, that man was stubborn, very stubborn. No one should be so stubborn."

I couldn't believe my ears. In a hoarse whisper I asked, "Then what did you do?"

75

"Nothing. I didn't do anything. . . . but Comrade Albino shot the preacher. Oh, he was stubborn all right. Then Comrade Albino said, 'See, their God didn't rescue them. No one can defeat the Shining Path. *We* are the future. . . .' Yeah, we're the future." I heard something change in Rico's voice—not so boastful, not so sure. But after a moment's silence, he added, "That's why Pastor Jorge in Santa Rosa better take note."

To my surprise, Rico jumped up off his mat and ran out of the hut . . . but not before I saw tears roll out of his eyes.

❖ ❖ ❖

Two days later the guerrillas were preparing for another raid when Comrade Albino yelled at me. "Alfredo! Get your jacket, and here"—he shoved a rifle into my hands—"it's time you made yourself useful."

"Forgive me, Comrade Albino," said Rico, stepping up, "but the latrine is nearly overflowing. I thought Alfredo might be able to clean it out today. Isn't that being useful to the revolution?"

The commander scowled. "Yeah, I guess so." Then he gave me a hard look. "But that latrine better be emptied by the time we get back. And next time you're coming with us."

By this time the camp had two pickups and a beat-up sedan. All twenty-three guerrillas climbed into these vehicles and roared off down the road. I was left in camp alone.

As you can imagine, I wasn't very eager to clean out the latrine. I planned to have the job finished before the soldiers got back, but I wasn't ready for that stinking job just yet. I wandered around camp, poking my head into the different huts that had been built out of the old Inca ruins. Comrade Albino's hut was the only one that looked like a real building. It wasn't fancy, but he had a cot and a desk and a gas lantern. On the wall was a map of the province of Ayacucho. I studied it, finding the city of Ayacucho, my village of Santa Rosa, the villages of Anta, Pacchac, Chakiqpampa—where Rómulo Sauñe had come from—and finally Huanta. I stepped back, thinking about Rico telling me they had burned down a church there.

Comrade Albino had wanted me to come with them this morning. But would they be blowing up more churches? Would I be a guerrilla then? Rico had stepped in this morning so I could stay in camp. I didn't know whether to be grateful or embarrassed. Didn't he think I was old enough?

Next to the map on the commander's wall I noticed a poster. It was a drawing—a cartoon, really—of a mob of angry villagers stoning one poor man who was on his knees in the middle of the crowd. Across the top of the poster were the words, "The Shining Path leads the way!" The caption under the cartoon said, "No one escapes the will of the people!"

Was *that* what the Shining Path was all about—terrorizing and killing anyone who would not go along with them? It sure sounded like that's what happened at the church in Huanta. And here was a poster celebrating the same kind of violent mob rule.

❖ ❖ ❖ ❖

When the guerrillas returned the next day, they had another vehicle, a larger Ford truck—a real truck—with several sheep in the back. They were also waving new blankets and carrying bags of what turned out to be potatoes and corn . . . and some bottles of liquor.

Most of the men climbed out of their vehicles in a happy mood. However, three of the fighters had been wounded, one severely. He was carried to the commander's hut and put on Comrade Albino's bunk. But as soon as the commander entered, I heard him shout, "I told you to use my bunk, not get it all bloody! Pick him up and put a plastic poncho under him. And don't get any ideas about sleeping in here, either. As soon as Doc patches you up, you're out."

He stomped out, his face twisted into an angry scowl. Doc Alverez, the oldest man in the camp, went in. Doc was not a real doctor, but apparently he had had some experience with treating illnesses and mending wounds, because everyone considered him the best medical help in the camp.

From time to time we could hear the wounded man screaming in pain as Doc tried to help him, but when Doc finally came out two hours later, the look on his face announced that he had failed.

Comrade Albino began swearing and waving his arms and making threats about how he was going to burn down the whole village for killing one of his men. Pointing a finger at me, he yelled like I was the one who had fired the fatal shot. "You! Get up that hill and dig this man a grave! He was a true and noble soldier in the people's guerrilla army, and he deserves a burial with honor. . . . Well? Don't just stand there with your thumb in your mouth! Get moving!"

I didn't have my thumb in my mouth. I never put my thumb in my mouth! He was making fun of me for being the youngest person in the camp. Turning on my heel, I found the pick and shovel and went up to the growing cemetery.

Sweat ran down my back under my shirt as I dug furiously. After I'd been digging for about an hour, Rico joined me and began helping me dig the grave. We worked in silence for a while. Then he said, "Don't mind him. He didn't mean anything against you. It was just a rough day. Somehow the people knew we were coming, and several of the men had guns. They ambushed us from a bluff above the road just outside the village. I don't know where they got so many guns, but . . . Comrade Albino was just mad about that. Don't take it personally."

I gritted my teeth. Personally? How else could I take it? He didn't make such snide remarks about anyone else in camp.

Two hands made the work go faster. When we finished, Rico said, "You coming?"

I shook my head and waved him away as I turned my back to him and stared into the woods. A moment later I heard the crunch of his footsteps as he headed on down to the camp. I hated the camp. I wanted to go home to Santa Rosa. The guerrilla camp was no place for me. I wanted to be herding sheep on the mountainside and playing my flute.

Sheep. I turned and looked back down toward the camp. The sheep the guerrillas had brought were still in the back of the truck, bleating miserably. If I couldn't go home, maybe they'd let me care for the sheep. That would be better than being kicked around every day in the camp, being ordered here and ordered there to do everyone's dirty work.

I sank down on the pile of dirt from the newly dug grave, facing the trees, and pulled out my flute. I needed the music to soothe the raw places in my spirit. Then I heard noises coming up the mountain. I twisted my head and saw a procession of men carrying the body of the guerrilla who had died. Comrade Albino was near the front of the line. I leaped up and backed away.

"No, no. Don't stop." The commander pointed at me. "Our comrade deserves burial with honor. The music is fitting."

Was he making fun of me? But he waited patiently. So I raised my flute to my lips, and for the first time in a long time the notes came easily. I could remember the old songs. Maybe it was because I was playing for someone else and not just for myself.

When I had played a few songs, the commander spoke. He said the man had been a loyal soldier and how worthy it was to die for the revolution. Then the men lowered the body into the grave—respectfully this time. No one said a prayer or words from the Bible, just talk of the revolution. Fortunately for me, everyone helped fill in the grave as a means of honoring their fallen comrade.

Later that night, the soldiers slaughtered one of the sheep they'd brought back from their raid and roasted it over a fire in the middle of the camp. They opened the liquor and began hooting and boasting about how much they had taken from the village they had attacked. "Ha, ha! That old farmer looked so funny running after the truck, waving his fist."

"Huh. Shoulda shot him. He didn't bring the sheep like we told him to."

"Nah. He can't do us any harm. Besides, we got his sheep, didn't we?"

I glowered at the men making fun of a poor farmer. To my shock I heard the thoughts that were in my head come out of my mouth. "Seems to me like we're no better than the bandits who used to raid our villages."

A sudden silence fell on the group. Everyone looked at me, then at Rico, and finally at Comrade Albino. I was terrified. But it was true! I was glad I said it. It made me feel less like a boy . . . and more like a man.

But to my surprise, the commander broke into a great laugh, as if I'd told a joke. "Yes, but we're bandits for the revolution that will someday set them all free!" Just as suddenly, the laughter faded and Albino glared at my brother. "*However,* Comrade Rico, you better make sure your *baby* brother understands that."

Chapter 9

Dynamite Jorge

Some of the older fighters tried to bully me because I stayed at the base camp all the time, but Rico came to my defense. "If you had a younger brother here, you wouldn't want him going out on raids, either. Leave him alone."

"What good is he if he's not going to fight? Why don't you send him home to be with his mama?"

"What good is he? I suppose *you* want to clean the latrines and herd the sheep. I'm sure that could be arranged."

I appreciated Rico sticking up for me, but it sure was boring staying in camp all the time. "Why can't I just go back home?" I asked him when we were alone.

Rico shook his head. "You know why you're here. We got caught in that fire fight back in our village. I pulled you into the truck to keep you from getting shot. But, now . . . if you went back, you might be suspected as Shining Path. You wouldn't be safe."

I just stared at him. I felt trapped. Was I going to have to stay here forever?

A couple days later when the commandos returned from a raid, all the soldiers seemed to avoid me. I looked for Rico but couldn't see him. Had something happened? I began to panic . . . and just then I saw Comrade Albino walking toward me. He stopped and looked me in the eye, almost kindly. "I'm sorry, son. Comrade Rico was a good fighter. An army patrol caught us, and he got hit. We . . . would have brought back his body for an honorable burial, but the army called in helicopter gunships, and the fighting was too intense. We had to get out of there."

The blood felt like it had drained out of my body. My brother . . . dead? Not Rico! My mother . . . oh, this was going to kill her. What was I going to do without Rico!

I stood rooted to the spot where the commander had left me, too stunned to cry. Several guerrillas patted me on the shoulder as they passed, carrying their gear to their huts. Then I was left standing alone.

Finally I willed my feet to move and wandered up to the graveyard. I stood there looking at the graves, two of which I had helped dig. Now there wouldn't even be a place to put a cross marking Rico's burial place. Worse still, had *anyone* buried him? Or was his body lying under some bushes by the side of a mountain road, waiting for the buzzards?

My eyes were drawn to the woods behind the graveyard. Was there a trail in there that might lead somewhere? I had always wondered but never checked it out. I wandered into the trees, my thoughts scattered. Without Rico, I'd either become the boy everybody picked on, or I'd have to go along on the raids and prove myself as a guerrilla fighter. Could I do it? Could I actually shoot someone?

I had heard all the revolutionary speeches about fighting for freedom and equality, about tearing down the corrupt government in Lima and defeating the cruel army. Some of those speeches sounded good— but to me the Shining Path seemed to spend most of its time intimidating poor village people. I'd only spoken my mind when I said that they didn't seem any better than the bandits who had lived in these hills before them.

I kept walking, wondering what I was going to do. My father had been killed, and now so had my brother. I was the only man left in the Garcia family from the village of Santa Rosa. I remembered the times on the mountains when my brother would chase me as we played hide-and-seek among the rocks. My eyes filled, and I could hardly see the trail I'd stumbled upon. Whether it was an old Inca path or an animal trail I couldn't tell and didn't care. It was taking me somewhere . . . somewhere away from the Shining Path.

On and on I walked, over one hill and around the next until my legs felt like a couple of fence posts that I could hardly make move anymore. It was getting late when I stumbled over a small stone and tumbled down a steep slope, stopping with a crash against a crooked old tree.

My neck and shoulder and hands felt like they were on fire. At first I thought a poisonous snake or maybe a scorpion had bitten me, but the burning was everywhere my skin was not covered by thick cloth. When I looked back up the hill, however, I saw the cause of my pain: I'd rolled through a patch of stinging nettles. I knew the plant well; it had a thick, leafless stalk covered by what looked like silver velvet. The "velvet," however, was made of glasslike splinters.

Maybe I was fortunate, because my tumble stopped my aimless wandering. I sat under the tree and picked the flaming hairs from my skin by what little daylight remained. Below me I could hear the gurgling of a brook, but I knew its cool water would not help ease my pain until I plucked out the source of the burning. Each time I thought I was done, I'd move a little and feel the sting of another nettle brushing against my clothes.

By the time I had regained comfort, it was too dark to travel farther.

The cold night air pressed down on the mountains like an invisible icy hand. I needed shelter. I found a hollow between a couple of rocks, but their cold surfaces sucked the warmth from my body like a winter wind. I needed a thick blanket, or better yet a small fire, but there were no matches in my pockets, no steel and flint.

I stood up and hopped around. My teeth were chattering, and I began to worry about freezing. What was I going to do? A long night stretched ahead of me, and I was already shivering. Pretty soon I realized that I wasn't able to see very well, either. Above me, the hilltops were clear enough—no clouds were coming in. In fact, a few stars were beginning to twinkle in the darkening sky.

But when I looked down toward the creek, it was as though a fog covered everything. It seemed to float and move like smoke, but there was no fire, no smell of anything burning. I looked up, then down, and up again. No, it was not my eyes. I could see just fine, but something was creating a cloud in the gorge below. Curious, I climbed down farther and farther until I was into the cloud, and then I detected the faint smell of rotten eggs—not very strong, but enough to take away my appetite.

When I reached the brook, the fog was so thick I could hardly see where I was going. And strangely, down in that gully the air around me seemed unusually warm. I reached down to scoop up some water for a drink and found that it was warm, almost hot. I almost laughed. *That* was the source of the cloud. That stream was fed by hot springs, and when the night air got cool enough, a fog rose from it.

The air was damp, but a huge stone at the stream's edge was warm enough that when I laid down on it, my shivering soon stopped. It was as though someone had answered my need, not with a thick blanket or flickering fire but with a warm sleeping rock. I felt like thanking that someone—God, maybe?

Instead, I pulled out my flute, blew a few tentative notes, and then a few more until I was playing the old songs that had kept me company while herding sheep as a boy. I played for my brother and played for my mother and I played for . . . well, for the warm rock, and then I went to sleep.

❖ ❖ ❖ ❖

The next morning, I climbed up out of the foggy canyon, taking care not to go through the nettle patch, and found the trail I'd been on the evening before. Hunger knotted my stomach, and I thought about going back to the Shining Path camp, but I had no idea where it was. I might have been able to retrace the trail to the west, but somehow I didn't really want to go there.

Santa Rosa had to be to the east, so I continued in that direction on the trail, not knowing how long it would take.

I hiked all day, but in the evening I began to recognize some familiar mountain peaks, and by nightfall I came over a hill and looked down on the small valley that contained my hometown. I wanted to run down the hill and straight home, but I remembered what Rico had said about people in my village:

would they think I was part of the Shining Path? So I crept into town quietly.

I was imagining a dim glow from the lamp and cooking fire shining through the window of our small house, so I was shocked at how cold and dark it looked when it finally came into sight.

Throwing all caution away, I raced past the last couple of houses, setting the dogs to barking. "Mama! Mama!" I cried as I stumbled through the doorway.

"Who's . . . who's that?" A weak cry came from my mother's small curtained-off corner.

My mother was lying on the floor, whimpering like a puppy. "Oh, Alfredo, my Alfredo, my Alfredo. Finally you have come home to me. Oh, my Alfredo."

Mama was sick—so sick that at some point when she had gotten out of bed, she had fallen to the floor and been unable to crawl back into bed. She had managed to pull some blankets down and created a heap of them around her on the dirt floor, trying to keep warm.

I felt desperate. How many days had she gone without a fire or water from the spring? When was the last time she had eaten? I helped get her back into the bed, tucked in the blankets, and lit a candle. Then I went outside to get some wood for the fire, but there was none stacked by the house.

"Mama, I'm going to be gone for a while, but don't wor—"

"*No,* Alfredo! Don't leave me again!"

"Shh, shh. It's all right. I'm just getting some wood and water."

"Get it from our neighbors! Don't leave me."

"I—I can't do that, Mama. I can't be seen around the village. The Shining Path might pick me up as a deserter. I'll just slip out of town to get the wood and water in the dark. I won't be long."

"No, no, don't worry about the Shining Path, my son."

"But, Mama! They have eyes and ears everywhere. I don't dare risk it."

"No," she said in a frantic voice. "The Shining Path does not come to Santa Rosa anymore."

I sighed. "Okay, Mama. I'll be back soon." I left, but I kept to the shadows and slipped out of town with my bucket. I wasn't going to risk being reported by some Shining Path spy.

When I came back, I made Mama some soup with some vegetables lurking on the larder shelves and some herbs she'd picked and dried. After the soup, she seemed stronger, so I asked what she'd meant by saying that the Shining Path didn't come to Santa Rosa anymore. "Are they afraid of the army that attacked the day Rico took me?"

Mama shook her head wearily. "No, no. They came back several times to find the person who had betrayed them to the army. Each time they . . . they killed someone." I longed to ask who. Our village is not so big that I don't know most people, at least by sight. But Mama didn't stop. "By then we had buried our old priest, and Jorge, the man who attended Rómulo Sauñe's Bible institute, became our pastor. He can preach better than the priest, and many

people have given
their lives to Jesus."
Her eyes, clouded with
sickness, seemed to
light up. "It's wonder-
ful, Alfredo. He has
taught us new songs,
too."

She paused, but I
said nothing. "But one day," she continued, "the
Shining Path came and gathered all the people into
the village square. I went because I wanted to see
Rico, but I couldn't see him.

" 'Who's the leader here?' they demanded. At first no one spoke, but then Pastor Jorge stepped forward, trembling, like he had the fever.

" 'Are you willing to accept the authority of the Shining Path in this village?' the rebels demanded. I could see that Jorge was afraid, but he answered in a clear voice, 'The Lord is my authority. There is no other.'

"The rebel commander laughed and turned to the rest of us. 'This man isn't fit to be your leader,' he said. 'We will make an example of him.'

"So they tied Pastor Jorge to a chair and attached dynamite to its legs. They lit the fuse and everyone ran for cover. *Boom!* The dynamite exploded, and we all began to wail with grief. But when the smoke and dust cleared, there sat Pastor Jorge, alive and un-harmed." A little smile flickered on her face. "As the people cheered and praised God, the terrorists fled the village. The Shining Path has never returned to Santa Rosa."

I gave Mama some more soup, feeding her with a spoon. Why hadn't Rico told me this story? Finally I said, "Do you think God protected him, or was it some trick?"

"It was *God*, Alfredo. Just like He brought you back to me tonight. That was God, too. And we should praise Him."

In a voice so weak and thin that it sounded like the wind blowing through a pine tree, my mother began to sing a praise song. It was not like the hymns that our old priest had tried to teach us in

church, hymns that sounded so Spanish, so foreign.
This was mountain music, a Quechua tune, thanking God with words from the Bible. I got out my flute
and played along with her. The notes came easily.

Chapter 10

The Informer

I was so relieved to be in a place where I was free from the Shining Path that I went up to *El Mercado Bueno* the next morning and sat on the bench as the villagers came to get their groceries or check for mail.

Most people seemed happy to see me. Some asked about my mother and whether I was going to be staying in town. Only Andrés Gordillo brought up the uncomfortable subject of *where* I'd been.

"So, Alfredo, they are saying you joined the Shining Path. Are you still part of the revolution?" He sneered the last word.

I shook my head and looked away. "I

didn't join. I was taken away . . . kind of kidnapped."

"Yeah, by that brother of yours. *He* was a member. Where is he now?"

I looked down at my feet, trying to think of how to answer. I had no interest in defending the Shining Path, but Rico was my brother, and I really missed him. "He's gone," I murmured.

"Oh really? Where to?"

I stood up. "Dead," I said as I walked away.

I couldn't really blame Señor Gordillo for asking questions, but I didn't really want to talk about Rico anymore. Of course, I had to tell people at some point, and the best way was to let the word spread. Gossip might get a few details wrong, but at least I wouldn't have to talk about it all the time.

Suddenly I stopped dead in the street. I hadn't yet told my mother that Rico was dead! The night before I'd been so upset about the state I'd found her in that I hadn't wanted to tell her. But I couldn't let her hear it by rumor.

I ran home and found Mama coughing in her bed. She seemed to be having trouble getting her breath, so I brought her a dipper of water and helped her drink it until the coughing calmed down.

I struggled with how to tell her the bad news. I didn't want to upset her. "Mama," I finally said, holding her hand, "Rico's not coming home."

She closed her eyes and nodded her head slightly.

"No, I mean he won't ever be coming home." When she didn't respond, I added, "He's been shot. . . . He's dead."

"I know, Alfredo. I know."

"You knew? How'd you know?"

When her eyes opened I realized that they'd lost their sparkle. "I didn't know for sure that he'd been killed, but I had accepted it in my heart. But you, Alfredo"—she raised up a little, desperately gripping my hand—"God has something else for you."

❖ ❖ ❖

I spent the following days caring for my mother and visiting old friends around the village. It was good to be home, but I kept thinking about what Mama had said, that God had something else for me. Pastor Jorge came to visit her a couple of times, and he sure seemed like a nice man. He prayed with her and read from the Quechua Bible. Mama really liked that and would sometimes break into a thin song when he read a verse she knew.

Various women from the village also came by to see what they could do. They felt terrible when they heard that Mama had fallen and they hadn't been there to help. Mama called them "women of the church."

"Why do you keep calling them women of the church, Mama? Isn't everyone in Santa Rosa from the church?"

"Yes, yes, it's the village church, but not everyone is active. I would go every night if I could. These women who come to see me, they would do the same. Other women . . . well, God is still calling them."

Jesus and the Bible and church had come to mean so much to Mama that I went to church one evening myself and sat in back to see what was so interesting. The music was great, so different from the old Spanish hymns. Pastor Jorge preached, and at the end asked if there was anyone who needed prayer. I knew Mama needed prayer—she wasn't getting well—but I did not go forward.

The next day I started preparing our field to plant potatoes. Mama had sold our sheep while I was away, but the money from that was almost gone. With both Father and Rico dead and Mama sick, it was entirely up to me to raise our food. The responsibility weighed on me like trying to swim with clothes on. Could I keep us alive? Maybe when Mama got better she could work on her loom again, weaving her bright blankets that sold so well down in Ayacucho. But Mama didn't seem to be getting better.

One day Señora Morales—one of the "church women," according to Mama—came by to see how Mama was doing. When she saw me, she said, "Alfredo, you are growing up so fast, and handsome, too.

"Just yesterday a stranger stopped by *El Mercado Bueno* asking about you. He wanted to know if you were in town and where you lived. Sounded like he had something for you. Did he come by to see you?"

"No. No stranger has come here." I swallowed nervously. A cold trickle of sweat inched down my spine. Who would be looking for me? "What did this guy look like?"

She shrugged. "Just regular, I guess. He wasn't Quechua, but he seemed to know his way around town."

"How did he get here? Was he driving? Did he ride a horse?"

"I don't know. I didn't see . . . Alfredo! What's the matter with you? You've broken out in a sweat. I sure hope you aren't getting sick with whatever your mother has!"

"No . . . no. I'm okay. Señora Morales, when did that man leave town?"

"I don't know. If he didn't come by here to see you, then I don't know where he went. I suppose he went back down the mountain."

"But did you see him go?" I insisted.

She looked at me strangely. "No. . . . Maybe he didn't have anything for you. I didn't see him carrying anything. Maybe he just . . . I don't know. Don't worry about it!"

But I was worried. There was only one reason why a stranger would have been asking for me: The Shining Path had tracked me down!

I thought about the guerrilla who had been shot as a deserter the first day I had arrived in camp. That seemed like a long time ago, like some other life, far away. I'd never heard where they'd caught him or whether he'd been given a trial, though I knew what kind of "trials" the Shining Path gave people. I'd heard them talk about what happened in various villages to people who did not cooperate. Once a person was accused, there was almost never any defense. Is that what had happened to the deserter? Is that what would happen to me when the Shining Path found me?

Once Señora Morales was gone, I told Mama about my fears.

"But, son! From what you've told me, you never really were a member of the Shining Path. You never went on any of their raids. You never shot at anyone, did you?"

"No, Mama. But that might not make any difference. Comrade Albino kept saying that he wanted me to go with them on their raids to prove my loyalty. It was only Rico who made excuses for me and arranged for me to remain in camp."

"You didn't take a pledge or anything, did you?"

"*No.*" I felt desperate. "But, Mama, they're after me—I know it. And it sounds like they've found me. They shoot deserters, Mama. They *shoot* deserters. And I ran away. Oh, Mama, what am I going to do?"

Mama folded me into her arms. "Don't panic, my son. God will provide something." She closed her tired eyes and rubbed her forehead. "I know," she said as she opened her eyes. "You must flee! Go down to one of the cities—Ayacucho or Chosica, or even Lima. There you can lose yourself among the crowds, and they will never find you."

I groaned. "I don't know, Mama. The Shining Path is just as active in the cities, and they've got ears everywhere. Probably that's why they came here to Santa Rosa. Someone here must be an informer."

"Not necessarily, Alfredo. After all, the Shining Path knew you were Rico's brother and that you were both from Santa Rosa. It only makes sense that they would come here looking for you if they wanted you. Maybe we should just trust the villagers to hide you." Her eyes glistened. "I could speak to Pastor Jorge. He could arrange it."

I sighed. "No, Mama. What you said earlier is best. I'm going to leave town. I wouldn't want to put you or anyone else in danger." What I didn't say was that I didn't trust the villagers not to report me. I had heard how the Shining Path got information. Sometimes they beat it out of people. But her mention of Pastor Jorge did give me an idea.

I stayed in the house all the rest of that day—didn't work in the field or go to the store or anything. But when darkness slid down the mountainside, I slipped out and made my way to the church. I found Pastor Jorge in the small house next door preparing some beans and tortillas to eat. I didn't feel like telling him where I was going or why, but I said, "I need some help, Pastor. I've got to go away for a while, and my mother is still too sick to take care of herself. Would you see that some of the women— some of the *church* women—stop by to check on her every day? And when I can, I'll send you some money."

"Of course, my son. We will care for your mother.

And . . . I'll pray that you have a safe and successful trip."

I was surprised. He didn't quiz me about why I had to go or try to talk me out of leaving. He just said he would pray for me.

✧ ✧ ✧ ✧

Back home I quickly made Mama and me something to eat, built up the fire, and threw an extra shirt and pair of socks into a small bag.

"Here, take my Bible, Alfredo, and read it."

I looked at the book she had pulled out from under her pillow. It was one of the Quechua Bibles that Rómulo Sauñe had brought to town. I didn't even know Mama had one.

Suddenly we heard pounding at our flimsy door. "Alfredo Garcia? Open up!"

I dropped Mama's Bible, grabbed my bag, and ran for the small window in the back of our house. I had just climbed out when I heard the door being smashed in and my mother scream. "What? The army! The army! What do you want?"

Without looking back, I scampered down the steep hill behind our house and ducked into the brush at the bottom of the ravine. I followed it for a short distance, thinking about Mama's last words. The army? How could it be the army? Why?

I was so curious that I climbed back up to the lip of the ravine and made my way to where I could see our house again. An army jeep sat in front of it with

its headlights shining at the front of our house. Two soldiers in uniform were standing beside the jeep, their guns at the ready.

While I watched, two other men came out of our house. My mother staggered to the door after them and stood there leaning against the frame for balance. I could barely hear her scolding voice. "Leave my boy alone. You have no reason to bother him."

Chapter 11

Rejoining the Rebels

The army jeep roared away from our house, its cloud of dust glowing red from the jeep's single taillight. I didn't even take time to go back and tell Mama good-bye.

All that night I put distance between Santa Rosa and me, trying to figure out why the army was looking for me. I had been so fearful of the Shining Path that I hadn't even been thinking about the army.

But it had been an army patrol that attacked the Shining Path the day that Rico was killed, and Comrade Albino had said they weren't able to retrieve his body. I had imagined my brother's body rotting under a bush beside the road, being pecked at by buzzards . . . but what if the army had picked up his body?

What if he wasn't dead? What if he had only been wounded? My mind began racing faster than my heart as I ducked under tree limbs and climbed over rocks. If he had been only wounded, and the army had captured him, he might be in jail somewhere needing my help. But Comrade Albino and the other guerrillas had seemed so certain that he had been killed. What exactly had he said? *They would have brought back his body for an honorable burial . . . but the army had called in helicopter gunships . . . the fighting was too intense . . . they had to get out of there.*

But if there had been a helicopter, they might have taken Rico to a hospital in time to save him!

The thing that didn't make sense, though, was why was the army looking for *me* now, nearly two weeks after the incident. If Rico was alive, he couldn't have told the army anything that would have made me a wanted man. Rico would have protected me. He knew I hadn't gone on any raids.

My mind played with the possibilities. On the other hand, if Rico was dead, and the army had his body—either from picking it up after the gunfight or because he had died in the hospital—the only reason they would have come to our house would have been to tell my mother. Though I doubted they would have taken the trouble. It was true that the government cared little for us poor mountain Indians.

So why was the army at our door asking for me?

I stumbled on through the dark night, able to see only by the weak light of a new moon. The only conclusion that made any sense was that there *was* an informer in Santa Rosa. I had been fearing a spy for the Shining Path, but what if it had been an informer for the army? Such a person might have seen me in town and, knowing that I had been with the Shining Path, reported my presence to the army.

Did they know I'd been held against my will? But I had spent a lot of time in one of the Shining Path camps. That might give the army reason enough to come looking for me. They might want me to help locate the camp and identify the guerrillas in it and where they came from. That would be valuable information for the army.

Without really thinking about it, I had been making my way down toward the city of Ayacucho. As Mama had said earlier, it was easier to get lost in a crowd than in a village. But now I didn't know who to hide from. Was it the Shining Path or the army?

❖ ❖ ❖

A day and a half later I walked into Ayacucho, tired and very hungry. The sun was just peeping over the mountains, and I easily slipped in among some of the local peasants bringing things to sell at the marketplace—black felt hats, bright ponchos and skirts, or carts full of produce. A cabbage fell off one cart; I snatched it up, broke it open, and tore off big chunks with my teeth. It wasn't my usual breakfast, but it helped ease my gnawing hunger.

In the marketplace I saw some boys—younger than me—who were shining the shoes of tourists. With a few of the coins I had in my pocket, I bought a can of polish from one of them. Then I found some rags in the trash in an alley, and I was in business. By the end of the day, I had earned enough to buy some food and pay one of the boys for letting me sleep at his house.

I was proud of myself, eking out a living on the street. Everything was going fine until one day while a couple of boys and I were shining shoes in front of a fancy hotel, the other boys seemed to just . . . disappear. Suddenly a squad of soldiers came running down the sidewalk toward me with their guns out. I didn't take time to gather my polish and rags or anything. Just took off as fast as I could.

Later, when I met up again with my shoeshine buddies, I asked them what happened. They shrugged. All they knew was that the army was looking for someone. How they knew ahead of time, I couldn't get them to say, but that was enough for me. I had to get out of there.

I bought a bus ticket to Chosica. But would going to another city be enough? As I rode along on that noisy old bus, crammed beside a crate of squawking chickens, I decided that I needed some protection.

But the only protection from the army that I could think of was the Shining Path! If they weren't after me, maybe they would help me. I hadn't been away from the mountain camp that long. Maybe I could connect with the guerrillas in Chosica and convince them that I was a guerrilla in good standing. If they tried to check me out with Comrade Albino and found out I'd run away, I'd try to convince them that I hadn't deserted; I had only gone to visit

my mother after my brother died. Surely they would understand me doing that.

It was not hard to find the Shining Path in Chosica. All I had to do was ask some boys on the streets. They directed me to a small house where I was admitted and questioned all morning. Finally I was taken in to see the local commander.

He sat behind a small table in a nearly bare room and looked over the notes taken by the man who had questioned me all morning. Finally the commander looked up at me. "So. You say you were with Comrade Albino's unit in the mountains over toward Ayacucho. For how long?"

I'd been asked that question three times already, but I answered politely.

"And why did you leave?"

"My brother was killed, and I went to tell my mother, but while I was in our village, the army came looking for me. They seemed to be everywhere in the hills around Santa Rosa, so I didn't dare go back to the camp—someone might have followed me—so I left and finally ended up here."

"How do we know this story is true?"

"You can check with Comrade Albino." I hoped they wouldn't, but even if they did, my story would hold up—except I hadn't *told* the guerillas I was going back to my village.

"We will. But if you are lying, you will be very sorry." He stared at me with lazy eyes that didn't blink. I hoped I didn't show any of the fear I felt. I *was* telling the truth, pretty much, but I didn't know what might ultimately happen about the desertion issue.

"Tell you what," he said, leaning back on two legs of his straight-backed wooden chair. "While we're checking out your story with Comrade Albino, I'll give you a little assignment that will give you a chance to prove your loyalty to the revolution. You interested?"

I nodded slowly.

"We've been having a lot of trouble with these evangelical Christians. They don't seem interested in liberation and won't support the people's army. They've been coming down out of the mountains and setting up churches in the cities. They won't vote the way we tell them to vote. They won't put up posters we need to display around the city. And they won't contribute to the cause. We've got to put the fear of God into them." He laughed at the idea of making Christians fear God. "Got to teach these trouble-makers a lesson, and the best way is to get rid of their leaders."

The tilted chair legs banged upright again as the commander got up, pulled open a drawer in the solitary file cabinet, and brought back a piece of paper. "Here's a list of the churches and pastors who've been giving us the most trouble. The first one on the list"—he pointed with his finger—"is a man named Rómulo Sauñe. He's here in Chosica. You can prove your loyalty to the Shining Path by eliminating him." His lips stretched in a smile, but there was no warmth in the smile. "I'll assign two young soldiers to you, but you'll be in charge of the mission. Though I'm warning you: they will watch your every move and report back to me."

The hair on the back of my neck stood up when the man mentioned Rómulo Sauñe's name. Not the pastor that showed *The Jesus Film*! But I kept my face impassive.

"Go to his church," the commander continued. "Get to know his routine, where he lives, when he's most vulnerable. You plan the hit. We have to make an example of him to all the Christians in the region. They can't oppose us."

I found my voice. "How much time do I have?"

"Shouldn't take more than a week. By then I'll have heard from Comrade Albino." The commander stared at me with those lazy eyes again and then waved his hand to dismiss me.

❖ ❖ ❖ ❖

"And that is why I came to your house last night," admitted Alfredo to Rómulo Sauñe as he finished telling his long story. He leaned forward on the sofa in the little room Rómulo used as an office, absent-mindedly picked up his coffee mug, and looked in. The coffee cup was still full—and cold.

"Here. I will get you some hot coffee."

Alfredo waved his hand. "No. No thanks." He had something important to say, and he needed to say it now. He took a big breath. "All last night after I left your house I could not sleep. I kept thinking about my life, about *The Jesus Film,* about Pastor Jorge, and what I had learned about God as a child. I knew it wasn't right—this revolution that has killed so many innocent people—and last night I felt that I was indeed fighting against God—just like you said. And . . . that is why I have come back."

Alfredo reached out with his toe and kicked his gun a few inches toward the evangelist. "I am not here to kill you. I only brought this gun to prove that I was a part of the Shining Path. I came because . . ." He couldn't help the tears. " . . . because I want to ask you to forgive me! I want to change my life and give my heart to Jesus. Can you . . . can you help me?"

Chapter 12

Ambushed

"Gladly!" said Rómulo Sauñe at Alfredo's request for help in becoming a Christian. His face seemed to shine with joy. The pastor read Alfredo some verses from the Quechua Bible that explained how Jesus had come to earth to live as a man and die for our sins, and how God had raised Him from the dead before He returned to heaven. Then he read the story of the jailer in Acts 16 who asked the Apostle Paul what he had to do to be saved. "This is for you, too, Alfredo. Paul said, 'Believe in the Lord Jesus, and you will be saved.' Do you believe in Jesus, my young friend? That He died for you?"

"I do, Pastor! I do!" Alfredo fell to his knees beside the

pastor, and the two prayed together as Alfredo asked God to forgive his sins. "I want to be a Jesus follower!" he prayed. "Help me."

When they finished, Rómulo got up from his knees, went into the other room, and told his wife and a couple of other people who were in the house about Alfredo's revelation. The Christians came in and hugged Alfredo. They laughed together, celebrating his change of allegiance from the Shining Path to the true path of light, Jesus Christ. No longer would he be Comrade Alfredo; now he would be a "brother," *Hermano* Alfredo.

Afterward, Rómulo sat down with Alfredo alone to talk about his future and how he was going to build a new life in Christ. While they were talking, Alfredo suddenly stopped and put his hand to his mouth.

"Oh! Hermano Sauñe, I almost forgot." Alfredo dug in his bag and pulled out a sheet of paper that had not fallen out when he dumped his belongings onto the floor. "Here is a list of all the churches and Bible institutes that the Shining Path plans to attack. I certainly won't be doing any of these hits, but . . ." His shoulders sagged. "I am afraid others will take up where I left off."

Rómulo read over the list that Alfredo handed to him. Deep concern creased his forehead. He nodded whenever he came to a name he recognized. "This is serious," he said. "It looks like they intend a major attack against the Christians."

"You are right. It's because they see Christians as

a major obstacle to the revolution."

"But why? Why does the Shining Path hate Christians so much? We do more to care for the poor than anyone else."

"That is true," said Alfredo with a shrug. "In my own town, my mother calls the Christian women, 'women of the church.' They do far more to care for the needy than the Shining Path has ever done. Huh. Maybe that makes the Shining Path jealous. But the real reason they are against you Christians"—Alfredo grinned—"I mean *us* Christians, is because they cannot intimidate us. Christians love the government."

Rómulo Sauñe held up his hands. "No, no, Alfredo. We don't *love* the government. It is a human institution—sometimes good and sometimes bad. The Bible does tell us to obey it, but it doesn't say we have to love it." Rómulo sat silently staring at the wall, as though it were a window into the past. "One day in 1984," he said wistfully, "word went out that the Shining Path was going to attack our village of Chakiqpampa. My grandfather Justiniano, who was a leader in the village and the pastor of our church, thought it was best to leave since he knew he would be a target. However, he left my grandmother, Toefila, behind to watch over the house.

"Instead of the guerrillas, however, government soldiers showed up, accusing everyone of supporting the terrorists. They specifically accused my grandmother of feeding and housing the guerrillas. Grandma Teofila admitted that, as a Christian, she fed anyone who came to her door hungry.

"That was enough for the soldier—who was actually drunk. He began hitting her and demanding to know where my grandfather was. When she said he was away, he and the other soldiers drove her from their home and set it on fire. Far from the village they beat and tortured that dear old woman for fifteen days, trying to get her to admit that she and my grandfather supported the Shining Path. Finally they left her unconscious in a field.

"The next day, when she regained consciousness, she staggered to her feet and walked for miles over rocky trails to reach the village. At first no one recognized her, her face was so bloody and swollen. But when they realized who she was, they took her to the hospital in Ayacucho. She finally recovered, but . . ." His voice trailed off.

"Maybe . . . maybe it would be a good thing for the Shining Path to defeat that corrupt government in Lima!"

The pastor shook his head. "No. You don't understand, *hermano*. In Philippians 3:20, Paul says, 'Our citizenship is in heaven. And we eagerly await a Savior from there, the Lord Jesus Christ.' No earthly government, no revolution—certainly not the cruel Shining Path—will bring us true peace. As you already know, the Shining Path is no better than the government. You see, there is more to the story. . . .

"Some time after my grandmother was beaten, the Shining Path warned my grandfather, Justiniano, not to preach to the young people. But my grandfather told them that he could not stop. He had to obey God rather than man, and the Bible told him to preach the Gospel.

"In December of 1989, everyone heard that the Shining Path was coming back. This time my grandfather decided he would not hide. He was eighty-three years old. What would they do to such an old man?

"On Monday, December 11, eight guerrillas galloped into the village and rode straight to my grandparents' house. 'Come with us, you leader of these miserable Christians,' they said. They dragged him out to a field where two hundred revolutionaries waited. There they beat him with clubs.

" 'Stop,' my grandfather pleaded. 'Can't you see that we are all brother Quechuas?'

"Several of the villagers begged that their pastor would be spared. But that only made the terrorists angrier. They cut out his tongue and held it high for everyone to see. 'We told you to stop preaching!' they said. 'Now you will stop.'

"They threw my grandfather to the ground, pulled out his beard, and finally stabbed him to death. 'If anyone buries this body, we will kill him, too. Let his body rot as a reminder of what happens to those who resist the revolution.' Then they rode out of town.

"But that was not the end. Before the day was over, the Shining Path had killed forty-five others in surrounding villages."

Alfredo stared in shock at Rómulo Sauñe. It was as though telling this story had drained all life from him, as well. Together they remained silent for a long time. Finally Alfredo said, "So what are we to do if we cannot trust the government or the revolution?"

Rómulo opened his Bible and showed Alfredo a verse. "I think the Apostle Peter put it in order in 1 Peter 2:17: 'Show proper respect to everyone: Love the brotherhood of believers, fear God, honor the king.' Our trust must be in the Lord, and the Lord only."

The pastor clapped his hands together. "However, the Lord has given us a brain, and that sheet of paper you showed me definitely says that my family is in danger if we stay here. I think we should move. I am going to take them to Lima."

"What . . . what about me?" asked Alfredo. He hadn't thought about what he'd do once he declared that he was a Christian. But the Shining Path in this town wasn't going to be happy that he defected. There'd be no excuses now.

"How would you like to attend a Bible institute in Ayacucho? I think you would be safe there if you stayed off the streets for a while." Rómulo smiled, a big warm smile. "And maybe someday you could go back to your village and help Pastor Jorge."

❖ ❖ ❖ ❖

The Bible institute wasn't a large school. It was only a small house where a few new Christians lived who wanted to learn the Bible. Various pastors and more mature Christians came by to teach Bible lessons every day. Some of the students worked at outside jobs, but Rómulo Sauñe arranged for Alfredo to work on packaging Bibles and other Christian literature to be distributed to the villages. This gave him something useful to do without going out on the streets where he might be spotted by the army or the Shining Path.

A few weeks later, Alfredo received a letter from Rómulo Sauñe. It was dated August 1992. After greeting him in the name of Jesus as "Hermano Alfredo" and asking how his studies were going, he wrote,

> Remember when I told you about the Shining Path killing my grandfather? Well, I was not able to attend his funeral. In fact, my whole family in Chakiqpampa was so terrified that they simply buried my grandfather without a funeral and remained quiet, hoping the Shining Path would not return.
>
> I want to go back to my village and gather all my friends and relatives and celebrate my grandfather's life and ministry. It would be a good witness to all the people in the area that the Gospel is stronger than death and that even the terrorists cannot silence us.
>
> I will be coming through Ayacucho on Monday morning, August 31, and I hope to use the pickup from the Bible institute to drive up to Chakiqpampa, so I will be stopping by there

briefly. I hope to see you and find out how you are doing. . . .

"Drive up to Chakiqpampa?" Alfredo didn't even finish the letter before his mind began developing plans. What if he could ride with Rómulo Saúñe up into the mountains? He could get out at the junction where the road divided and walk on up to his little village of Santa Rosa while Rómulo Saúñe continued on the other branch toward Paccha—the place where the road ended and he would have to walk on to Chakiqpampa. It would only be a visit, but he really wanted to see his mother and tell her what had happened to him . . . if she was still alive.

✧ ✧ ✧ ✧

During the next few days, Alfredo's mind was so full of plans that he could hardly pay attention to his studies—though he didn't know yet whether Rómulo Saúñe would let him go with him. And even though he didn't know whether his mother was still alive, Alfredo found several small gifts for her. The most exciting was a hand grinder that could grind both corn and coffee. It would make cooking so much easier than using the grinding stone she had always used.

But to Alfredo's surprise, on Monday morning several other people stopped by the Bible institute. Some were Christian friends Alfredo had already met, and others were relatives of Rómulo. They all were planning on accompanying him into the mountains for the family reunion. Five, six . . . seven men and women—would there be enough room for him? Would Hermano Sauñe even let him come?

But he needn't have worried. When Rómulo Sauñe arrived from the airport and the joyous hugs and greetings were nearly complete, Alfredo ventured his request.

"Of course you can come! I should have thought to ask you myself. There's always room for one more in the back of a pickup."

The ride itself was like a party as first one and then another person suggested a Bible song to sing, many of which were new to Alfredo. But he pulled out his flute and tried to play along whenever he could. When the pickup finally stopped to let Alfredo out, everyone waved and wished him well and said they would meet him at the junction the following Saturday at about noon.

Alfredo hiked up the road to Santa Rosa with as much eagerness as a *vicuña*—a baby llama—on a frosty morning. It was only six miles, and in a couple of hours he was walking into Santa Rosa with a smile on his face. But it was only when he actually saw the front of his house and a little smoke from the cooking fire curling out of the hole in the roof that he thought about the conditions under which he'd left home—army soldiers breaking in the door and demanding to know where he was. Would they still be looking for him?

At this point there was no way to tell and no way

to escape, either, unless he ran off across country again. He would have to trust the Lord.

"Alfredo! You are home!" his mother cried when he entered the smoky house in which he had grown up. She flung her arms around him and squeezed with reassuring strength. Maybe she *was* getting better. Then she pushed him back to arm's length. "Let me look at you. I do believe you've grown some more. You look good! For once you have a smile on your face."

Alfredo laughed. "Yes, Mama! I gave my heart to Jesus! I am a true Christian now."

Mother and son talked late into the night. Alfredo told her how he had tried to rejoin the Shining Path to avoid being captured by the army but how God had protected Rómulo Sauñe, who showed Alfredo that he was fighting against God by trying to kill His servants. Again and again, his mother muttered, "Praise Jesus!" as tears wet her cheeks.

✧ ✧ ✧ ✧

The next few days passed all too quickly, and soon Alfredo was saying good-bye to his mother and Pastor Jorge—whom he had quickly come to like— and other old friends from Santa Rosa. "I told Rómulo Sauñe that I would meet him at the junction by noon," Alfredo said. "I'm still attending the Bible institute, but I'll be back some day. You can be sure of that."

"Here, ride my old burro down to the junction,"

offered Pastor Jorge. "She'll come home by herself . . . I hope."

"No, no. It's not that far. I'll make it in time. Besides, once I get in that old truck I'll be so cramped that I'll be glad I had a walk this morning." Alfredo set off on foot, turning back only once to wave at his mother, who was still standing at the edge of the village in a brightly decorated red dress, a green blanket around her shoulders, and her black felt hat pulled down on her head.

Halfway down the road to the junction, Alfredo passed the rusted-out body of the old car that the bandits tried to steal from Santa Rosa. It seemed like the bandit attacks had been the beginning of a change to his whole life. At first things had seemed to go badly, but—as he had learned at the Bible institute—God worked out all things for good for those who love Him. Now Alfredo had a new life.

At the junction he waited nearly an hour before he heard the sound of an approaching vehicle. As the Bible institute pickup rounded the corner, Alfredo saw that it had more people in it than on Monday.

"Get in, get in," called Rómulo Sauñe, who was also riding in the back. "Did you have a good visit?"

Everyone talked joyously for a while, but after an hour or so the conversation died down as it was difficult to be heard over the wind and road noise while riding in the back. As the truck came around a sharp bend in the road, Alfredo felt the driver sharply apply the brakes. Those who could, looked around the side of the cab to see the road ahead.

"Roadblock!" everyone seemed to say at the same time.

Alfredo held his breath as he looked past a line of twenty-five cars, rusty buses, and trucks. At the front of the line, a dozen or so armed men were inspecting each vehicle, sometimes requiring the people to get out to be searched. The armed men did not have army uniforms; they had to be the Shining Path. As the pickup crept slowly forward toward the head of the line, Alfredo recognized some of the men from the camp where he had stayed.

He looked around. Should he jump out and run? What if there were lookouts with rifles trained on the stopped cars? Would he be shot if he tried to escape? Finally he decided to take his chances by staying with his Christian friends. Maybe they would not recognize him.

By the time their pickup reached the front of the line, Alfredo had counted nearly a hundred rebels hiding in the rocks above the road or searching the vehicles.

"Everyone out!" demanded one of the rebels, firing a burst of shots into the air to get everyone's terrified attention. "Men line up in front of the pickup. Women over there!"

Alfredo kept his head down. He remembered seeing this guerrilla at the camp.

"Give me the gasoline out of your truck," he ordered the driver.

The driver had started to comply when gunfire erupted back up the road by a bus that had been stopped. Everyone looked to see what was happening. One man, trying to flee, was shot down. Alfredo wiped his forehead, grateful that he had not tried to escape.

The passengers from the bus began screaming, "Please, please! Don't shoot. No, no, no!"

Suddenly one of the men searching the pickup yelled, "They have a pistol. Who owns this pistol? It is a police pistol. One of you is a policeman."

When no one answered, another guerrilla raised his gun and shot one of the pickup passengers in the chest. In shock, one of the other men jumped forward to catch his falling friend. He was shot, as well. Then all order disappeared, and the terrorists began shooting with their automatic weapons at the line of men in front of the pickup.

"Cease fire! Cease fire!"

Alfredo had fallen to the ground with those around him. He didn't know whether he had been hit or not, but that voice giving the cease-fire order was familiar. Alfredo raised his head slightly and peeked over his arm to see a man in a camouflage army jacket and matching cap. Comrade Albino! The commander was going from body to body.

Just a few feet away, the rebel leader rolled over one of the dead with his foot, then knelt to inspect the body. Alfredo winced. Rómulo Sauñe! The terrorist commander stood up. "We got him!" he yelled into his handheld radio.

In the distance, the *whap, whap, whap* of helicopters could be heard. Comrade Albino looked up at the sky and shouted, "All right! Let's get out of here before the army arrives!" Then, just before he left, he turned and pointed directly at Alfredo. With his hand in the shape of a gun, he squeezed down his thumb and said, "Pow!"

Chapter 13

Onward Christian Soldiers

Four of the men who had been riding in the Bible institute pickup were killed in that attack. Many more from other vehicles also died.

Three days later, people streamed down from the mountains into Ayacucho to attend the funeral of Rómulo Sauñe, probably the most well-known of those to die that day. After the service in the El Arco church, over two thousand people created a parade that wound its way through the streets of Ayacucho.

PORQUE PARA MI EL VIVIR ES CHRISTO
Y EL MORIR ES GANANCIA

Alfredo boldly marched beside a woman in the front of the procession who carried a huge banner on which a verse was painted: "For me to live is Christ, to die is gain." They sang "Onward Christian Soldiers," and Alfredo played his flute loud enough for all to hear. Often they were joined in singing by many of the hundreds of citizens who lined the streets.

But not all of the onlookers were singing. Alfredo locked eyes with someone he had seen only three days before. This time the man did not wear a camouflage jacket and cap but was wrapped in a striped red, blue, yellow, and black blanket. On his head sat a brightly colored knit wool hat with earflaps. Commander Albino looked like any other harmless Quechua sheepherder just come down from the high Andes slopes to honor a beloved evangelist.

After the march, Alfredo went to the police station, uncertain whether he would be arrested or not. Nevertheless, he had some important information to report.

Within a month, the government captured the gang that had conducted the ambush that killed Rómulo. Within another two months, the government rounded up nearly twenty-five hundred guerrillas, including Abimael Guzmán, the leader of the Shining Path, and several of his top lieutenants.

Alfredo never told anyone what he had reported to the police. He only studied twice as hard. The best way he knew to honor Rómulo Sauñe was to get as much Bible knowledge as he could and return to his village—not with guns or revolution, but with the Gospel of Jesus.

More About Rómulo Sauñe

On June 23, 1992, the World Evangelical Fellowship gave its first ever Religious Liberty Award to Rómulo Sauñe, a humble Quechua Indian pastor from the Peruvian Andes. Christians from Africa, Asia, Europe, the Middle East, Latin America, and North America gathered in Manila, Philippines, to honor him because of his courageous ministry while his life was threatened by Communist terrorists. These terrorists had already murdered his grandfather, assaulted and beaten his grandmother and left her for dead, burned down his family home twice, and destroyed his church.

In an attempt to take over the South American country of Peru, these same terrorists, calling themselves the Shining Path, murdered at least twenty-five thousand people according to the U.S. State Department (some estimates go as high as one hundred thousand). They massacred thousands of Christians, including some eight hundred pastors, often wiping out whole congregations. Thousands of other civilians (the U.S. State Department estimates ten thousand) were caught in the crossfire and killed as the Peruvian military—sometimes ruthlessly—tried to stop the terrorists and capture their leader, Abimael Guzmán Reynoso.

Ten weeks after Pastor Rómulo received his award in Manila, he traveled to his childhood mountain village of Chakiqpampa, where he encouraged the Christians and visited his grandfather's grave. On September 5, 1992, as Rómulo drove back down to the city of Ayacucho, the Shining Path set up a roadblock and attacked again, this time killing Rómulo, his brother, two nephews, and several other people. When the guerrillas checked the bodies and found that they had killed Rómulo Sauñe, one radioed to his commander, "We got him!" Then they left.

Rómulo Sauñe had been born on January 17, 1953, in Chakiqpampa, where as a young boy he herded sheep on the steep mountains and learned of his Inca ancestors. Through his mother's side of the family, he may have descended from the royal Inca priesthood. Nevertheless, first Rómulo's uncle and then his grandfather, Justiniano Quicaña, accepted the Gospel of Jesus and became Christians. Other family members followed, including young Rómulo, until there was a thriving church in their village, a church that sent out missionaries to all the surrounding villages.

In 1978, realizing that the denominational divisions between Christians, introduced by various outside mission organizations, hurt the Gospel witness, Rómulo led in the formation of TAWA, a joint mission association, which many churches joined to restore unity among the Christians. One of its first projects was to work on translating the Bible into the Quechua language. This task was completed on September 3, 1987, and within a short time forty thousand copies were sold to the people.

Whereas the early missionaries had taught the people old English hymns in Spanish, Rómulo worked on getting the churches to accept new Scripture songs in Quechua written to traditional music with flute, pipes, and guitars. Young people eagerly embraced the change.

In time, Rómulo became a pastor of the pastors, guiding and encouraging them as the Shining Path became more and more violent, especially persecuting Christians, because they would not join them in their violence.

Rómulo's death, however, did not go unnoticed. Braving the threats of the Shining Path, two thousand people paraded through the streets of Ayacucho singing "Onward Christian Soldiers" and carrying banners declaring "Ayacucho for Christ" and the Bible verse, "For me to live is Christ, to die is gain."

One week later, government agents finally captured Guzmán and his top lieutenants, bringing an end to the worst of the Shining Path's reign of terror (though the organization still exists and sometimes launches terrorist attacks).

Since Rómulo Sauñe's death, his brother Joshua has stepped forward to pick up the ministry. Joshua is now the leader of an association of some two hundred Quechua Indian churches. In addition, Rómulo Sauñe schools have been set up in the Ayacucho region to help care for some of the fifteen thousand orphans created by the Shining Path.

For Further Reading

Whalin, W. Terry and Chris Woehr. *One Bright Shining Path*. Wheaton, Illinois: Crossway Books, 1993.
Strong, Simon. *Shining Path: Terror and Revolution in Peru*. New York: Time Books, 1992.

For more exciting stories from Dave and Neta
Jackson, read any of their four *Hero Tales* collections.
Here's an excerpt from *Volume IV*:

JOHN G. PATON

Missionary to the South Sea Islands

John Paton quit school as a young boy because of a cruel
schoolmaster. But he was determined to become a missionary,
so he studied at home.

Born into a fine Christian home in Dumfries, Scotland, in
1824, John saved enough by the time he was twelve to pay for
six weeks of private schooling. He continued to work his way
through school, university, divinity school, and medical training. Finally, at the age of thirty-four, he was ordained by the
Presbyterian Church of Scotland and commissioned as a missionary to the South Sea Islands.

On November 5, 1858, John and his wife, Mary, arrived on
the Island of Tanna in the New Hebrides, a group of eighty
islands now known as Vanuatu, about fifteen hundred miles
northeast of Australia.

Other missionaries had established a solid work on Anatom, a southern island in Vanuatu, and several of their converts
accompanied the Patons north to Tanna. At first the Patons felt
overwhelmed by the warring cannibals of Tanna. Then they

realized that the Christians from Anatom had been just as savage only a few years earlier.

The Tannese people worshiped and feared many idols and had no concept of a loving God. Witches and wizards in each village cast spells they claimed controlled life and death. They stirred up the people to drive out the missionaries.

Warfare between tribes worsened, with some of the worst fighting happening right outside the Patons' house.

Three months after arriving on Tanna, Mary Ann Paton gave birth to their son, Peter, but she became sick with fever and died on March 3. Their son also died from fever less than three weeks later. Paton was so shaken by these tragedies that he could hardly continue.

Not long after this, white traders—who also hated missionaries because they discouraged the natives from buying rum and muskets—deliberately sent three sick sailors among the people to spread measles, knowing that the witch doctors would blame Paton. The epidemic killed a third of the people, and the survivors sought revenge.

Two local chiefs protected Paton for a time, but that only increased the intertribal warfare. Soon Paton was running for his life, protected for a while by one chief, only to be chased by the same tribe the next day. He almost certainly would have been killed and probably eaten if a passing ship had not rescued him.

He had been on Tanna less than four years.

John then spent nearly two years speaking to churches in Australia and Scotland, raising financial support and recruiting more missionaries. One of those recruits, Margaret Whitecross, married John and returned with him to the islands in 1865.

John longed to settle again on Tanna, but the mission board assigned the Patons to Aniwa a few miles east. Superstitions on Aniwa were just as godless, but possibly because the island was smaller, there was less warfare and cannibalism. As the Patons learned the language, they slowly gained the people's confidence and were able to present the Gospel until nearly everyone on the island became a Christian.

In his later years, Paton traveled widely on behalf of missions until his death on January 28, 1906.

DEDICATION
Passing Up the Good to Achieve the Best

~~~~~~~~~~~~~~~~~~~~~~~~~~~~~~~~

Young John Paton attended the school near his home in Dumfries, Scotland, and did well enough in his studies that his teacher took an interest in him and secretly gave him a suit of clothes. However, the man also had a terrible temper that exploded whenever one of his students displeased him.

One day after the teacher savagely beat John, he begged his mother, "Please don't make me go back. He whips children for no reason."

His mother looked into the incident and knew John had been treated unfairly, but she said, "You still need your education, John, and we cannot afford to send you to a private school. Give it one more try."

So John returned. But the moment the teacher saw him, he went into another rage and kicked John. In pain and terror, John ran for home.

Even though he was younger than twelve, there was nothing else for him to do but help in the family business of weaving stockings. He worked from six in the morning until ten at night with only a half hour off for breakfast and lunch and an hour off for dinner. But John did not waste those spare moments. He studied his lessons and saved his money so he could go to a private school.

John had already given his heart to Jesus and dedicated himself to becoming a missionary, and he knew that would require a good education.

Once he had saved enough, he enrolled in the Dumfries Academy for six weeks. Then he went to work for a surveying company that provided a shorter workday than helping with the stocking weaving at home. He studied during every available moment, including his lunch hour. His supervisor noticed the twelve-year-old's seriousness and offered him a promotion and special training if he would agree to serve the government for seven years.

"Thank you, sir," said John. "That is most kind." Then he stopped and considered. After seven years, he would be nineteen but not very far along in his preparation for mission work. "I'm sorry, I would agree for three or four years, but not for seven. That would put me too far behind in my preparations."

"Preparations for what, lad? Why would you refuse an offer that many gentlemen's sons would be proud of?"

"Because I have already dedicated my life to another Master."

The supervisor frowned. "And who would that be?"

"To the Lord Jesus," responded John, "so I must prepare as swiftly as possible to serve Him as a missionary."

"You fool!" the supervisor roared as he lunged toward John. "Accept my offer, or you are dismissed on the spot!"

John stood his ground. "Forgive me, I know you mean only kindness, but I cannot delay the purpose of my life. I cannot accept."

The angry supervisor paid John for the work he had done and fired him on the spot.

A less-dedicated youth might have gotten discouraged. But even though John was still so young, he went to the City of Glasgow, where he worked for the Presbyterian church part time as a visitor and tract distributor. Later he served as a street evangelist for Glasgow City Mission while he worked his way though the University of Glasgow, the Reformed Presbyterian Divinity School, and Andersonian College for medical training. Finally he felt ready to be a missionary.

꒰ ꒱

Dedication is being set apart for a special task.

FROM GOD'S WORD:
The Holy Spirit said to them, "Set apart for me Barnabas and Saul to do a special work for which I have chosen them" (Acts 13:2b, NCV).

LET'S TALK ABOUT IT:
1. Do you think John was wise or foolish not to accept his supervisor's good job offer? Why?
2. It might seem *good* to go to the beach on Sunday morning, but it's *best* to go to church and worship God at that time. Think of two examples where you might have to give up something *good* in order to achieve the *best*.
3. Try inserting your names in the Bible verse above. For what special work has God chosen you?

RESOLVE

"It's God's Decision Whether Cannibals or Worms Eat My Body!"

~~~~~~

Many church leaders tried to convince John Paton to remain as the pastor of Green Street Church in Glasgow, Scotland, by telling him how useful he would be there. They even offered him a nice house and a larger salary, but he knew God had called him to the South Sea Islands.

"But the cannibals," warned an old gentleman. "You will be eaten by cannibals!"

He said it so often that John finally responded, "Mr. Dickson, you are old, and your body will soon be laid in its grave to be eaten by worms. What difference does it make if cannibals eat my body? Why should I save it for the worms? Isn't it more important to live and die serving and honoring the Lord Jesus?"

John had already resolved that since he had only one life to live, he was going to live it for Christ and leave the time, place, and means of his death in God's hands.

This freedom from the fear of death was essential on the Island of Tanna, where witch doctors often tried to kill him. One day, when the tribal wars were raging, Paton held a worship service in a village.

"We don't need your God," said three powerful witch

doctors. "If we ever get a piece of food you've eaten, we'll use it to kill you with magic."

"You think so?" said Paton. He then took some plums and called to the whole village, "Watch me eat this fruit."

He took a bite from each of the three plums and gave the witch doctors the remainder. The village people looked on in horror as the witch doctors began their magic rituals, wrapping the leftover fruit in leaves, burning part of them, and saying curses over them.

"What's taking so long?" said Paton. "Stir up your gods to help you! I'm not dead yet. In fact, I'm perfectly well!"

Finally they stopped and said, "We must wait until we call in other witch doctors to help us, but you will be dead within a week!"

"Very well," Paton said. "I challenge all your priests to unite in trying to kill me. But if I am still healthy a week from now, you must admit that your gods have no power over me and I am protected by the true and living God!"

Every day that week, the witch doctors blew their conch shell trumpets, rallying all the priests on the island to work their magic against the missionary, but on the next Sunday, John was healthy and strong as he stood before the whole village.

"My love to you all, my friends! I have come again to talk to you about the living God and His worship," announced Paton. "Come and sit down around me, and I will tell you about the love and mercy of my God and teach you how to worship and please Him."

Two of the witch doctors sat down with the people, but the third one, a very large, strong man, went off and came back with his spear.

"Of course he could kill me with his spear," said Paton to the crowd, "but that would not prove that his magic had any power. And if he does kill me with a spear, my powerful God who protected me from his magic will be angry with him."

For weeks thereafter, that witch doctor followed Paton

through the jungle with his spear held high, but God prevented him from ever throwing it. John Paton, in the meantime, left the results in the hands of Jesus.

꒐

Resolve settles a matter so that you are not continually troubled by it.

FROM GOD'S WORD:
Choose for yourselves today whom you will serve. . . . As for me and my family, we will serve the Lord (Joshua 24:15, NCV).

LET'S TALK ABOUT IT:
1. What did John Paton mean when he asked Mr. Dickson, "Why should I save [my body] for the worms?"
2. How did Paton have the courage to challenge the witch doctors to try to kill him by magic?
3. Tell about a time when you resolved to trust and obey God. What challenges did you face? How did your resolve help you face those challenges?